If this then that

New stories, new writing Vol. 1

Selected, edited & introduced by

S A Harrison

First Edition: Published by
WriteSideLeft

September 2018

CW00953156

ISBN: Print: 978-1-9998181-4-2

ISBN: eBook: 978-1-9998181-5-9

Stories by the Authors listed

Selected & Introduced by S A Harrison
Cover Design & Photo by Robert Golden

Published by WriteSideLeft Ltd, UK

www.writesideleft.com

Contents

Introduction

The short story form is nearly as old as the language, *all* language ancient or modern. Fable, spoken tale, short myth, allegory, excerpt or sketch, its history stretches back and back.

This anthology is an experiment: a collection of new writing that tries to set up a conversation between stories and their authors and generations. Which piece did elder or younger write? Which is written by a newcomer, which by a seasoned author? In what genres?

The title is an invitation, an ironic nod to today's technocratic world: shouldn't life be getting easier, follow a more logical orderly path for all citizens of the world? We're better connected than ever before. If I prune the tree for her, she'll be happy? If I alter my body I will be understood and loved? If I build a cabin, eat the right food, welcome strangers, do everything I'm told, (or my shrink suggests), be there at the right moment, tick the right boxes to help the search engine algorithms—the sunny safe uplands are mine and ours? What could possibly go wrong? What are our excuses now? Fate? Greed? Laziness? Media-fatigue? And the prologue story, is it standing as an avenging discarded angel, warning us?

The stories are surprises: 'Do you have a story about the unintended consequences of human connectedness?' I chanced. I hoped for and got a superstore of variety. I believe that has contributed to the unexpectedness of the anthology, that it is more than the sum of its parts. Questing, poignant, cautionary, darkly funny, satiric, tragi-comic, romantic, ironic, battling with identity and memories, melancholic, dystopian, generous or horrifying, reinventions, nightmares, wry asides at the #me-ness of #now: all sorts are here. Some are excerpts from longer works or works-in-progress — characters may pitch up more than once.

The writers and the order of play: As anthologiser I wished to sweep aside the authors, to disembody and anonymise them, to focus simply on their writing and imaginations. Then I wanted to join their hands in a seemly narrative order. Naturally, I threw the printed stories in the air to see how they landed. Several times. As I pondered. And pondered. Eventually, I glanced up at my bookshelves to see the reproachful begetter of a deal of resented agonising young time spent: *Paradise Lost* (and *Regained*). Turns out, Milton came in handy. Welcome to the world of IFTTT. (S A Harrison 2018)

Prologue: Watch the Show

E Ruby

I have spent my life looking through a lens or twisted mirrors. When I learned to see, they gave me a kaleidoscope you could fill yourself. I put gravel, shards of glass: complete shit in the chamber and filtered it to something pleasing that I controlled with my hands. I've never liked the stillness of life. I've never liked the memories that tune in.

'So, when we get in there he's already got half his kit off.'

'Jesus.'

'Yeah, well, she's a lot more filthy off-camera. And we put the beers there. They don't always bring beers. It's like, what do you call it? A trope? It's like a paedophile's trope.'

'Pedo-brand beer. Pedo-brew.'

'Brewed in an NBC basement by a forty-year-old called Dave.'

'It's not really a skill. Using bits of punctuation to make faces like a real person. And crap grammar. It's not a skill.'

'Is if you can lure a freak into a rental house.'

'And it's always the same house. If I saw that house I'd think, shit, they're onto me, back to the dark web, or whatever.'

We pulled into that familiar drive. Anthony thrusted the gearstick and winked.

'First thing you need to know about this job. Everyone is stupid.'

My dad bought a state-of-the-time camcorder to watch a little boy grow up. I got caught then, and now I'd probably say it wasn't me too, unrecognizable in mittens and smiles and pixels. But dad still sits, thinking the motes and notes of the dusty cassettes are the same person. Stupid.

Tripping out of the van, I realized the camera lead had become entwined, taut around my neck.

'Careful! You break it, you pay for it. This isn't bloody CNN. We're doing real work here, catching real predators.' Sideways smirk to his colleague. 'Gotta keep the pervs on their nerves.'

8

Anthony was always coming up with little catchphrases. I'd catch myself doing it too. When I bumped into Dave from the basement, who pretended to be an underage girl, I told him to *act the teen, keep 'em keen*. He laughed but he looked tired, his mind just jumbled lower cases and capitals.

I was ten when I got my first camera. Not a point-and-click; I didn't like the stillness of life. I knew that the truth would change after the picture; the people would stop smiling and the rows would start again. Mine was a stocky, awkward thing and let me keep life rollin', incognito. I took videos of the calms before the storms before the rain beat us up. I crouched atop the stairs to catch mom's face slipping as the front door slammed. I once took a video of a bird, broken, jagged and dwindling, because that was real.

My life set me up to mark a sharp division between the stupid and the smart.

The NBC gig was ironic because I'd landed my first job by filming perfect little girls happy, little girls playing, little girls playing with perfect plastic women which I read later gave them dysmorphia, or dyscalculia or something *dys-similar*. After I stopped catching predators I saw a girl with body issues. Once when she was awkwardly trying to cover her breasts, her stomach, her thighs after she got undressed, I thought about that article and how playing with Barbies fucked her up, but I couldn't remember it right, so we just had sex, my mind on my cock, groping at her insecurities.

Life set us all up, really. I can't talk. I used to think the adverts for sports drinks would make me better at soccer. I was still picked last.

Jed, my half-brother, hooked me up with TLC.

'Acronym for tender loving care?'

He shrugged, said he doubted it, and later mailed me a contract. The presenter was called Wilson; he was ten minutes late to pick me up. It was Fall, and the leaves on the pavement were skeletal and seeking their own company.

'Any luck, we'll find some old smut in this hole.'

'Why would you want old smut?'

'It's funny. Women back then had bushes the size of like, actual bushes. We had a man once, down on the Shore. Wouldn't get rid of his son's porn after he died.'

'That's so sad.'

'Yeah, so lame, I think he wanted to look at it. Too embarrassed to buy titty mags but happy to live in his own shit. These people, no respect. No dignity. Embarrassment. Let's rock and roll!'

The old van shuddered but didn't move. His fists pounded at it. He was an angry person.

'They're killing themselves. Can't live like that, how can they live like that?'

It sputtered back to life. 'There we go! It's the engine. Should have been given an upgrade. Six fucking years. What you say?'

'They're killing themselves.'

He chuckled, and I noticed his cheeks looked like cold plastic stones on the banks beneath his dry eyes.

'Long as people want to watch 'em die, I don't give a rat's ass.'

Reality TV. In reality, the divisions between the smart and the stupid are blurred. They have room for lapse and insecurity, so we, the master chefs, carve reality up into neat, nibble-able pieces.

There, in the gardens, dry grass quivered. I got good at telling where our target was because the yards were like shanty towns; a necropolis of things that expired just after their warranty. Posthumous microwaves. Electronics, obituaries their peeling labels. That stillness of death. Lukewarm co-presenter straddling a washing machine.

'Cold bitch. Butter wouldn't melt. Did I tell you about the butter guy? Not just butter: food, perishables. Butter was green, for God's sake. Still would though. She might be cold, but I'd still wreck her.'

There was a fly, struggling, trapped against the lip gloss she had smothered that orifice with. 'Will, where the hell's your make-up? Darlin', some of us gotta look normal in this freak show.'

I faded into the background. Watched the show. Him, so coated in bronzer that he looked like a collectable penny. Her trying to turn her face into a face.

'Both of you, positions. We're rolling in...'

'New blonde, Jan? Curtains match the drapes?'

'Five—'

'What curtains? Eugh!'

'Four—'

'It's not gonna keep him interested.'

'Three—'

'Hire another prostitute, go on, shithead.'

'Two— '

'Rather that than bone you, aging bitch.'

'One—smile, you're on air!'

And then it was all *Good morning America we're live from Jersey, Guttenberg. Today we're giving you a man with a truly heart-breaking story! That's right: Will, two-times cancer sufferer Martin complains that he can't watch TV because his home is so cluttered – can't watch TV imagine not being able to see this beautiful woman every day aww! You hear that folks, isn't Wil just a sweetheart anyway? Let's meet this week's Obsessive-Compulsive Hoarder.*

I pressed stop because I was meant to. The smiles trickled, and the odious reveal was complete. Wilson slapped me, hard, on the back.

'Get ones where he's crying or freaking out. Might find some decent loot here, but I wouldn't hold my breath. Actually, probably would hold my breath, these people are fucking animals!'

I was there for two years. I felt guilty at first because I wanted to hold the hands of these sick, lonely people, but the network had a little team, each with a BSc in commiseration which allowed them to make soothing sounds in their victims' directions. And I had a tiny secret. From every dilapidated hole, I'd snatch a bent tin opener or a newspaper from the early nineties. It was my way of saying sorry. And while I couldn't give them back, I put them in a box in my wardrobe, under the suits and shirts I was slowly amassing. There they were cared for, not in the blind, desperate way they had once been. But it was something.

Once the reel is done, it's a piece of evidence that needs to be defiled by itching fingers.

I had a contract with Springer in March. I lurked at the back and controlled the swinging cameras like a guillotine at some toothless man who most certainly was not the father until the tests came back and then he most certainly was the father. Once, on stage, our gracious host offered a man who had been battered by reality a job, working here, amongst the stars. I saw him a month later, cleaning the bathroom. I asked how much he was being paid.

'This is an internship.' He looked down at his mop, the toilet, his life.

I quit.

Drinking uptown, someone told me I had a good face. I didn't know what a good face was. 'It's the face the people want to see,' she told me: Janice, older, and the drapes were fraying, and the carpets were moth-eaten. But she saw me as a kind of protégé when I'd satisfied her enough. So, after a handful of lessons from a man who did the voiceovers for dog food commercials, I felt like I was ready.

The other side of the lens.

And I fucking hated Bonnie. She wasn't clever, she was stupid. She was lucky. Every time she made a stupid, uneducated guess she'd guess right, and another counter would slide down. I could feel the contrast of panic between us oscillate—needles in a tornado. Stupid, lucky Bonnie. Shameless emotional slut. I was being raped, forced to force myself into a derision of her gratuitous, ugly joy. I would grab her pudgy hand and squeeze and sigh with relief, the only genuine relief I got, but still false because my

14

sigh was intertwined with the groan when she screwed up. Then the penny dropped. She screamed and I, tending to the rapine of my mind, screamed too.

I would love to go back: just a decade, maybe less. Before I knew that security was a snip-snip away, in an even deader thing inside its torn mouth.

Me and Jed were at a strip club.

'Get into porn,' he told me, looking around and feeling inspired.

I laughed. 'No way. I have a reputation.'

'Your reputation ended when those anti-Semitic comments went public.'

'Jesus, that was out of context.'

'Just film it. You don't have to be named, shamed, credited.' He grabbed the nearest girl by the waist, two more whiskeys, no ice, no please.

So.

We never really had a chance. We were lied to from the get-go; the first time our parents sat us down outside a bright box and we thought, 'that's it, that's life, yup'.

And now I'm here.

This is not a narrative.

This is the 4 am slot; the dead hours.

This is an amalgamation of all the men who told stories around fires.

This is the slap-chop. It cuts vegetables faster than you ever could. You dickhead.

This is a fusion of the great poets who learnt how to craft without hands.

This is the 'smart' mop. Any stain, anywhere, anyhow. Even the stain of your own dumb carbon.

Look at what we turned narrative into.

A game show to see who can dance best on writers' graves.

A competition where we can vote for the dreamer we ridiculed the least.

This what we do now: we bask in the ashes of the greats.

With open eyes.

I think I'll go upstairs tonight. I'll go to my wardrobe. I'll find the box of rescued items. I'll take them into the backyard with some lighter fluid. The rest you can probably guess.

You're not as stupid as we thought you were.

Paradise by Numbers

S A Finlay

How could a man not be beguiled by the gentle shh-shushing of the petite siren waves, on a sultry day on the shore of a volcanic black sandy beach in St Lucia, an hour before sunset? His feet standing so close to the equator, at the centre of everything? His legs tanned, his torso so muscled at fifty(ish)? His bespoke silk trunks hollering, 'pineapples and palm trees galore!'? Bronzed neat-haired chest stuck out to welcome the heat, arms folded across as he dipped manicured toes in and out of the warm water? His straw-hatted head of glossy brown hair bent to peer for tropical fish beneath the surface, and a rose-coloured paper parasol-ed rum cocktail screwed carefully into the sand a metre away, steel drums panning reggae behind? A blind date in Paradise. Guaranteed outcomes. What was not to smile at? And yet George frowned.

He checked his phone. Not for the time; to see if he'd got sand in it—not his best idea bringing it to the beach even it was waterproof, and it made the pocket of his trunks sag a bit—which he didn't imagine to be alluring to an approaching prefabricated meticulously planned love-story. Truthfully, he knew what time it was: the sun set early in this Eden, the crickets, locusts and tree-frogs chittered on palms and walls, as chameleons shuttled across hot stones. The sky would darken in the blink of an eye—and George's eyes tended to blink a bit often and a bit fast. She was due to meet him at the shoreline at five o'clock. It was five minutes past. He didn't mind. He viewed the lateness as fashionable and useful, might ponder his future a while, even if five minutes wasn't a lot.

Ezgi—that was her name. He remembered just as she snuck up on the crunch-less sand, sashayed into view, tropical sarong billowing in the warm slight breeze that blew her long, long legs into full sight. Scarlet-varnished toenails glinted maybe a bit menacingly at him. Her hair, all that glossy dark hair, swaying about sculptured shoulders, huge brown eyes smiling, delicate bangled arms reaching out, a string bag in the crook of one, a neat bikini-topped décolletage stuck out invitingly, like the deal of the day on a local market stall. All vanilla and cinnamon and exotic spices. She was shaking him by the hand, flinging herself about him in a vast expectant hug. She bashed him with the bag.

'Et in Arcadia ego!' he muttered, returning the embrace a bit awkwardly. She was nearly as tall as he was.

'Eh?' she said, gaily.

'Nothing!' he replied. 'How lovely to meet you. How was your flight? Are you settled?'

'Ooh yes! I slept and dreamt. The Engagement Suite is gorgeous. All flowers and fruit. Though I heard something scuttle! I don't much like the creepy crawlies.'

'Oh dear,' said George, a bit stuck for words, even if he'd practised vacuous romantic chat in front of the mirror. (He'd also tried hugging with a pillow.) 'Well, I guess there are a lot of tropical scuttlers hereabouts.' He sank his feet further into the sand, leant over to get his cocktail and slurped it through a candy-striped straw. The paper parasol twirled about and caught him on the nose. 'Ouch. Oh dear, my parasol is scuttling a bit now. Do you have a drink?'

'I fear so. It's all so kind of you. Do we get guests? No no no, I don't drink. We don't drink!' she said, a look of tut-tutting and, 'you failed to memorise the spec,' all over her gorgeous face.

'I think they rent a crowd for us,' he said, matter-of-factly. Did she not know this already? The exquisite detail of it all?

'*Rent*! Eurgh!' she exclaimed. She reached in her bag for a bottle of water and sipped it. She pulled out her mobile phone. 'Do you mind if I report my successful rendezvous to the Agency?'

'Good idea. Not at all. I'll do the same,' said George. 'It's *our* rendezvous, after all,' he added, attempting a small amendment of perception and emphasis, betraying a tendency to remind and correct or a desire to be *assertive*.

They stood there, side by side, heads down, eyes averted from the beautiful private view of sun and sky meeting sea. She couldn't help it, she had to 'tell my friends I'm here!' and take a selfie. She didn't invite him to feature in it, so he decided to be at one with her and affect to text someone, (anyone really?) simultaneously. A few minutes passed. George sipped his drink and waited.

'Well, it's all just perfect!' she said when she'd finished. 'You look quite manageable. What odd eyes you have. I'm off for a swim in the pool! Shall I see you later for dinner? Sun sets ever so soon, and I don't much like the dark.'

'Yes, yes. Of course. I think I'm quite manageable. Do have a swim. I don't much go in for pools. As you know. What time would you like to eat? Between seven and eight, you said?'

'I think eight would be perfect. I could rarify myself for you. We've done so much together already, after all.' She winked.

George blushed. No, they hadn't really. It had all been games. Online. Clever enough. He ought to know. 'You're already as rare as clean water!' he said. Bingo! His first chivalrous compliment and he felt quite the besotted Bridegroom, like a true potential life-long lover and soul-mate ought to feel.

'Hmm,' she said. A look of doubt crossed her face, her mouth grinned white teeth, her eyes were vacant.

He blinked furiously, tried again, 'My blue diamond!'

'Oh dear,' she muttered, 'all mined out, don't you know? Never mind, I'm off. See you at eight.' She swished away.

George didn't know what to do with his three hours. He watched the sun go down, although the sun didn't really perform that whole *visibly setting like jelly thing* hereabouts. It didn't sink and squish and demise in a glorious graded time-lapsed riot of blood oranges; it just switched itself off—it was a *blink and you'll miss it* affair, and of course, George blinked rather a lot even when wearing sunglasses. When it was dark, he tiptoed to the poolside bar, listened to the steel drums a while, scanned the plashing water for his fiancée. He heard the giggling and gurgling and chittering of monied Americans, Brits, Chinese, a few Europeans. He downed his drink, went to his Groom Suite and lay down.

He tried to banished thoughts of Sally. They had a habit of creeping up and scuttling in on him, skin-shedding, shape-shifting chameleons, there they were before you spotted them. Well, she was long gone: he recognised the fleeting scintillating memories simply for what they were: anticipation and valediction. And fear. All perfectly natural. He felt a bit sick. Not to worry. The Agency had told him to expect it. And Ezgi had been warned. Ezgi also knew that his fantasies tended to go awry, abstracted and disinterested. She'd insisted she wasn't bothered so long as she got a husband, baby and citizenship. That was the quid pro quo. A carefully preselected gene-pooling, a result, and a *happy ever after*. Ideal circumstances and geography: a laid-back reggae and rum-fuelled (moderated to ensure procreation) Shangri-La, at a *menu prix-fixe*. Now that he thought about it, Ezgi didn't seem at all prenuptially jittery.

Why should *he* be? They were the fool-proof match, after all.

There were some half dozen other couples at dinner. George sidled in tugging at the itchy collar of his shirt. A waiter leapt out, escorted him to his 'sea-view corner seat, bees-wax candle-lit table.' George scanned the room—all the tables had sea views, and all had candles. He sat down. An ice-bucket with a bottle of champagne smooth-landed in front of him, a napkin glided into his lap, a flute filled with fizz nudged into his open hand. Smiles and winks and nods and efficiency. He knocked back the first glass and waited for Ezgi.

In she floated: that hair swinging about, a silver purse glinting in her hands, a beaded maxi dress slit up the side to within a centimetre of an invisible knicker line. He wondered if she wore underwear. He wouldn't blame her if she didn't. Even with the aircon, it was too hot, and he suddenly suffered the claustrophobia and surfacing sweat of the overdressed at an opera.

'Oh, I do love a man who dresses properly!' she said, planting a kiss on his forehead as she flounced into her chair, fluttered her napkin about, waved the glass of champagne away and reached for the jug of water.

He felt like her grandfather. She was younger. Fortyish he supposed — one wasn't permitted to know these days. Fair enough.

They ordered — Agency recommended — sea-food, followed by more sea-food, followed by fruits. George liked eating and he found the emporium of cocktails on offer 'enormously colourful fun'. He got stuck right in, rolled up his sleeves and dived into the platters of shellfish, and bream and bass. And slurped his drinks. Ezgi pulled a rictus of a grin as if from a bag of tricks, picked at her food as delicately as she might, and watched George. Now and then, she sighed, as if to hint at some disapproval of his voracious appetite or abominable table-manners. They ate mostly in silence; he munched away merrily, she sipped and forked the odd piece of fish without damaging her lipstick. Until a lobster claw flew across the table and hit Ezgi in the eye. She looked up from her phone.

'Ouch! Ouch! Fuck! Ouch!'

A waiter zoomed in. George dropped his lobster and leant across to her, handing her his sea-food grimed napkin. The candle guttered and died.

'Good grief! I'm so sorry! I got a bit over-excited! Are you ok? Does it hurt?'

'Well, of course it does, you idiot. My eye won't stop watering. What happens if I have a scratched cornea?'

George leant back, thought a moment, and offered, 'I don't think it'd affect the looks of our son?' Then he added, by way of suddenly remembered apology, 'Nor yours, I imagine?'

The waiters retreated as if fleeing a front-line.

'Well, that's a fucking relief on both counts then!' his fiancée replied.

The other diners swivelled their heads in dismay, set to messaging their complaints to The Agency. *Not good enough! Profanities in our Promised Paradise. Beautiful Wedding-Eves trashed.* Thousands of miles away, Compensation Computations started grinding out, all but audible as the steel drums rolled out a discreet lament.

'Have you finally finished eating?' Ezgi said, a hand over her eye. 'You need to take me to the sanatorium right now! I should only be going there to confirm I'm pregnant. I'm so angry!'

'Right. Of course! I'll just finish this lobster,' said George.

'You will do no such fucking thing!' Ezgi stood up, towered over him, wailed, caught the table-cloth, pulled it from under him. Plates and glasses crashed everywhere. Waiters dashed in. Diners dropped their smartphones and stood up to get a better view.

'Right then,' said George staring at the mess of his dinner suit. 'Let's go my darling.' He went around the table, took her by the shoulders, picked up her bag and phone, ushered her swiftly out, held her to him as he marched her carefully up the solar-lighted path, around the corner, up another path, behind the Bridal Bungalows, towards the neon-lit Sanatorium.

'George! How nice to see you!' said the friendly doctor of similar height, looks and age as they entered the pre-treatment room.

'Tom! Fancy seeing you here!' said George, a bit sheepishly. 'This is where you ended up?' he added, and as if prompted, shot an arm up protectively around Ezgi.

'You know each other?' wailed Ezgi.

'Yes, yes, from way back. His ex and I were colleagues,' said Tom. 'Now let's get you sorted. Sit down, there's a girl and let me take a look at that eye.'

George and Tom shook hands on the Sanatorium veranda, agreed to keep in touch, exchanged contacts. Tom winked at George, said things *like he was happy and relieved for him, wished conjugal felicitations, looked forward to seeing them again in the blink of any eye, ho ho ho*, the sort of banter that Ezgi

26

didn't seem to hear, understand or want to attempt, as she stomped impatiently from one bejewelled foot to the other and looked on with one unbandaged eye.

After George had seen Ezgi to the porch of her Suite, offered to come in and tuck her up and tend to her, (rebutted with an almighty huff and slap across the face and a 'see you tomorrow then, with my Now. One. Good. Eye.') he beat a retreat to his room. He lay down on his vast bed in his dirty suit. He slept long and deeply and dreamlessly. Sally didn't come to haunt him in the night. He awoke refreshed, if smelly, and ready…for what was to come.

At sunrise, the happy couple stood together under the festooned wedding gazebo. Ezgi wore a diaphanous floating maxi dress, her hair up, a white orchid clipped into one side, one eye made up, the other patched in yellow silk that flaunted her flawless complexion. George wore a cream linen suit, a pink silk shirt (undone at the collar), his un-socked feet in new navy-blue boat-shoes. Behind them, seated in teak steamer chairs, the diners from last night, the waiters, the match-making managers and staff. Further back, the steel-drummers at the ready. In front of all, right where sand touched sea, a bare-footed Canute in a frothy long silk coat, the Celebrant of indeterminate gender, raised its arms palms up to signal a beginning. The drums hummed. The crowd sighed and hushed themselves.

'A minute-long ceremony to establish a lifetime of mutuality and trust and general gorgeousness. Here we all are. Listen to the endless turquoise sea, feel the sun beating gently on your necks and the hot black sand in your toes, touch the sultry air with your fingers, watch the infinite blue sky, smell the blossoms, hear the cicadas, taste the salt in the wafting breeze. Merge the endless possibilities of your senses and minds: Join these two in harmony and…Take your pictures, here we go: three two one…Done!'

Smartphones turned towards the couple, or back to the selves, glinted in some ecstatic unison.

'Are we married? Is that it?' said George.

'Didn't you read the bloody spec?' hissed Ezgi.

The crowd dissolved, the chairs disappeared, the drums silenced. The Celebrant tip-toed off.

They stood there a moment, the two perfect newlyweds. Ezgi sighed, pulled out her phone. Messaged her incalculable number of friends.

'I think I'll go for a swim — your doctor friend said I could if I kept my head above water.'

'Of course!' said George amiably. 'Always keep your head above water! Would you like a kiss?'

'I don't think so. Let's do all that later, shall we? It's all guaranteed after all.' Ezgi said, pleasantly enough now, a flirtatious jutting of the hip, a newly-wed sort of grin across her pretty face, a merry promising glint in her chocolate brown eyes—or one of them anyway. She pranced off, waving, 'See you at eleven sharp in The Suite!'

George sat down on the hot black volcanic sand, removed his boat-shoes, shuffled on his bottom to the shoreline, let the warm water lap over his toes, shh shh his beleaguered heart. Attempted to imagine himself beguiled and convinced. He scanned the heavenly horizon. He closed his eyes. And he thought of Sally.

The Fall

G Cadwallader

He'd been half-dreaming about the storm when they were woken by a pine branch crashing against their bedroom window. No damage was done, but he had been startled. After he'd laid back down and switched out his reading light, his heart was still racing.

'Work for you to do in the morning,' Mary muttered before she fell back asleep.

He lay in the dark imagining how it would have been to live as a cave-dweller on a night like this. Then his cave was under the sea, everything swaying this way and that, the gale still raging underwater. A giant sea-branch flew past him. A freckled lobster —

it spoke in Mary's voice, but he couldn't make out what it was saying—hung before his face, its protuberant eyes adjusting to keep him in focus as it shook its head slowly back and forth. He was cold, chilled all down his right side. He was now on a sailing vessel, sea water pouring across the deck, his face covered in spray so that he could hardly see. The mast cracked behind him and the sails were falling down in a great snapping darkness when he woke up, shivering, half out of his bed sheets.

He opened the bedroom door and Mary's little terrier, Maisie, scampered in and leapt up to snuggle against her breast. To the extent that Maisie could be thought to be property she was jointly owned, but she had a way of letting it be known to whom she belonged. He would have liked to give Maisie a tickle under the chin, but the two of them were already snoring lightly.

He had particular pairs of trousers and boots he liked to wear for garden work and a golf cap from Sanibel to keep sharp twigs away from his eyes. He walked out to the front of the house, as he did early every day to take in the view and give a silent prayer of thanks to the sun or just as often to the rain. When his work had brought him to North Carolina, twenty years ago, he'd had no idea he would find such contentment amidst these rugged, thickly forested mountains. Right on cue, the coyote he saw each morning came trotting around the hairpin below the house and stopped in the road to look at him, as it always did, with its head dropped to one side. Surely it must recognise him, but it gave no sign. Day after day he nodded or waved a greeting to it but had received only baleful indifference in return. They stood about thirty yards apart like this for maybe a minute each morning before the coyote resumed its lope, along the far side of the road, swivelling its head so that it never lost eye contact, on its way to check out the Crampton's trash further up the hill. These were, he often thought, the most wonderful moments of the day.

He walked round to the back of the house, where the pine branch lay on the patio beneath their bedroom window. It was as long as he was tall. A couple of long thin holly branches had fallen into the box hedge. They were easy enough to pull out and drag to the fire pit at the far end of the yard. The grass was strewn with fans of conifer branches of every size from smaller than his own hand to the size of their breakfast table. The wind was still gusting strongly, brushing smaller debris across the lawn. He thought he should have had breakfast before he started work — a cup of coffee, at least — but there was so much for him to get done.

Across the sidewalk that ran along the side of their yard, a tree had come down, a birch tree thin enough for him to cut up with his own chainsaw. He filled up the oil and put on the heavy gloves he used with the saw and pushed his wheelbarrow round the front of the house onto the footpath. He heard himself whistling and knew he was happy. The tree was covered in ivy. It ran up the trunk like external ventricles designed not to breathe or nourish but to suffocate. The saw cut through the ivy like sponge, biting into the muscle of the tree. He loved how the saw worked its own way through the yielding wood, turning the trunk into its teeth in a spiral embrace. He loaded up the barrow with the foot-long logs and pushed it back to the log-store. As he turned into his yard a great gust from behind seemed as if it might lift the barrow off the ground. It was exhilarating to be out so early in such a gale. He laughed out loud. After he'd finished unloading the wood and cleaning the saw, his hamstrings where he'd been bracing himself were pinging like nine-irons and his arms and back were feeling sore in just the way he liked. He felt good and thought he'd shower before his coffee. Mary was not in the house, she must have gone to the grocery store. He stripped off in the utility room and walked naked through the house and stood under the shower, much hotter than he'd have run it if she was home. In the shower, he had a strict routine of shampoo, with his favoured chestnut-colouring conditioner, soap and scented body-wash, which always included a pause, while the conditioner soaked in, to marvel at how something so close to drowning could be so rejuvenating.

When he got down to the kitchen, Mary was home. The fishmonger had got fresh lobster in. He remembered they'd talked about it the day before. He loved lobster.

'I'm going to treat us to lobster salad for lunch,' she said.

He kissed her hair before assembling his mug, the fine-ground Pike Place coffee and paper filter. Out of the corner of his eye, he caught the blue plastic bag shift on the counter. His heart skipped, then sank. Something was writhing inside the bag. Mary must have seen the look cross his face.

'The fishmonger insisted I take it live. He said it'd be ten times better this way.'

She emptied the black, crimson-specked lobster into one of the sinks. It scrambled around, testing out the sides of the sink with its toes, like we might test the sea, he thought.

'He said they can be killed painlessly,' she said.

He peered down at it, scratching away more frantically now. What did this creature have to do with a fishmonger, anyway, he wondered, with its interrogating eyes and articulated limbs? A fish might flap around a bit, but could it really be said to be trying to escape?

He looked up how best to kill a lobster. In his early forties, he had eaten lobster on five continents, but had never before been asked to kill one first. For the most humane method he trusted the English, and sure enough, there it was on the BBC website; push the tip of a large sharp heavy knife through the centre of the cross on the back of its head. It was 'believed' to kill the lobster instantaneously, that was as far as the BBC's Food Guide would commit. First, though, he was supposed to freeze it into somnambulance.

'How can freezing it be painless?' Mary wanted to know.

It was a good question.

'Anyway, we don't have time,' she said. 'I've already got the water boiling. It's lunchtime.'

He thought he might put it in the freezer for ten minutes. They paced around the kitchen watching the clock, imagining the lobster slowly freezing. He asked Mary how she would want to be finished off by a giant alien towering over her with a blade half the length of her body.

'Swiftly,' she said.

He took it out after seven minutes. The lobster wriggled in his hand as though it thought it had just had a lucky escape.

Together they searched for the cross.

'It must be this, here,' said Mary, pointing to a division in the lobster's shell.

He was doubtful. He held the lobster's head with his large heavy knife poised over it. The lobster was going to die, he reasoned. He might as well try to make the best of it. Trying not to look away, he pushed the knife in. He had expected a simple thrust through uniform lobster flesh, but the knife splintered the brittle shell, then there was an inch of firm flesh, followed by a chewier, gristly layer. The lobster flexed its legs, arching its back to look up at him. Perhaps it was already dead, and these were just post-mortem electro-chemical spasms. But it was difficult to believe that this was instantaneous death. A squirrel Maisie had cornered in the garage had scratched in the air with its legs like this, screeching in pain and terror. He had hit it three times with a spade and then sat in his study for half an hour, fighting back the tears. When he went back to bury the squirrel, it had disappeared. He thrust the knife in again, as swiftly as he could, swivelling it left and right. After several heaves of its chest, the lobster finally slumped and was still.

While the lobster boiled away, Mary cut up the salad ingredients. He told her about the tree he'd cleared.

'The ivy is taking over,' she said, 'dragging the trees down.' She was engaged in an open-ended war on ivy. 'It's going to pull those birches down onto the greenhouses. Maybe after lunch we should go out and cut it down, if you can face more cutting after the trauma of the lobster.'

She was teasing, but it stung. He didn't see why, after he'd gone out with his saw and cleared a tree before even the dog walkers were up, his manliness should be compromised by a lobster.

Mary had mercifully taken the sweet, pink meat out of its shell. Though the salad looked fabulous, he approached it like a murderer returning to the scene of his crime.

With what he hoped was the restrained dignity of a public hangman enrobing himself, he retrieved his plaid flannel shirt from the laundry hamper, and put on his work trousers, gardening boots and cap. He took the wheelbarrow loaded with his secateurs, a pair of long-handled loppers, made in Germany, his chain-saw and thick gloves out to the greenhouses. Mary followed with Maisie running between her legs.

'She ought to be on a lead,' he said.

With the loppers, he reached a little above head-height and snipped through the ivy that grew about as thick as his gloved thumb. He made two cuts on each cord, about eighteen inches apart, ripping off the lengths between and throwing them in the barrow. A few of the cords were much thicker, climbing like hairy pythons up the trunk. He worked through these in a moment with the chainsaw. His arms quickly tired, working the saw above eye level, and he needed to take a breather.

'You should use a ladder,' Mary said.

Some men would have been happy to quit at that point, content to let the ivy above the gap turn crisp and brown over the coming weeks, but this would spoil Mary's view from the kitchen window. He wanted to be thorough. Besides, he'd seen ivy throw down new tendrils and re-root itself, resuming its upward growth with regenerated vigour. With the chainsaw, he cut another gap, closer to the ground, where the growths were as thick as his arms. Then he got the ladder and climbed up into the higher branches, cutting out huge clumps of green growth and throwing them down to the ground. The first tree was done to a round of applause from Mary, and he took a little bow.

'I think I'll just do one more,' he said feeling the soreness in his glutes and triceps.

'What about the others?' Mary asked.

They'd have to wait.

He worked his way up and down the trunk of the second birch. He stripped off his jacket and cap. When he revved up the chainsaw, Maisie started running around under his feet yapping. 'Best take her inside,' he said.

Mary coaxed Maisie away and they headed off towards the house. 'Hold on,' she called back. 'I'll be straight out.'

He waited on the top step of the ladder for a few moments but didn't much like the way it wobbled in the wind or how the branches groaned, and anyway he was almost finished. He had enjoyed the applause and liked the idea of surprising Mary when she returned. He wanted to feel in full the admiration he felt he'd earned, that had been diminished by the encounter with the lobster.

He reached up into the densest part of the ivy, clipping the sinews away with deft strokes of the saw, reaching up with his left hand to strip a long thread away from the bark. A huge clump of leafy ivy came away from the tree into his face, toppling him backwards off the ladder. As he fell, he felt the chain-saw slip from his hand. As he landed, he heard the ladder clatter to the ground. He had fallen onto his knees and shoulder, then the right side of his head. He felt, rather than saw the tree twist out of the ground, its ivy scaffolding no longer tethered but acting as a great sail, lifting and then falling in a spiral. He wanted to get up onto his hands, but there was a huge pressure all around him. He was cold, his bones felt cold. He continued to fall. As he sank it grew darker and everything around him grew still.

There was something he wanted to say to a lobster, but it never came.

The pressure in his head was unbearable. He had grown so cold that he knew he would soon start to shiver, but he never did.

Passing Friends

G Frosh

The legs had always been her best feature...at least so Wally had said. She'd been quite something in those days – up the Lyceum, aglow with the magic of the dancing, the glamour. But Wally was no more, and her calves not as shapely. Like broomsticks now, they disappeared into the pink housecoat, itself without form, shapeless as an empty shroud, or washing hung out on a murky day.

This morning, however, was warm and sunny, but the paleness of her skin, the bluish pallor, seemed to him to impart a chill, to make him shiver, almost. As the sun came from behind the clouds, the housecoat took on some substance, the sharp angle of her hip defined by the new shadows. Her back towards him, she stooped to attack the pavement outside number 59. It was a bit manic really, her fury at other peoples' fag-ends, the angry broom jabbing towards the gutter. Not six months ago she'd been on forty-a-day herself.

Of course, he could guess where the anger came from. All those pills, lining the mantle above the gas fire.

Maybe there had been talk of getting engaged, but Wally had gone off to the Royal Artillery, down Woolwich, and had never reappeared. Even though it was wartime, there didn't seem to have been an official telegram, not a stiff 'we regret to inform you'. There was simply a sense of…'well…he didn't come back.'

But that was more than sixty years ago, and in spite of all the loving detail, about this job, and that job, there seemed to have been no more Lyceum. And there she was even now, at number 59, where she'd lived since she was just eight years old. Maybe because there was no more dancing, and no intimations of blossoming, certainly no scuffling in the stationary cupboard, she'd continued to live as her parents had sternly prescribed — rules laid down when she was maybe only fifteen. If you got involved with boys, they'd warned, the next thing…well, you'd get in trouble, be ruined...it was bound to happen, they'd said.

She was not exactly prim, but clearly, there had never been anything relaxed in her contact with men, maybe even back then, dancing. So, he was quite taken aback when she first asked him. Apparently, she was 'getting a bit of gyp', and asked would he put on a Belladonna plaster for her? The plasters, apparently, were a fool-proof solution — her Mum had sworn by them, and her Aunty Eileen. Though not familiar with the remedy, he was happy to oblige, just as he had been to pick up bits of shopping for her or change the odd light bulb.

Nevertheless, he was still a bit surprised and even more so when he saw the size of the plaster!

Her scullery, a confusion of extraneous tables and chairs, sideboards, footstools and loungers, was even gloomier than normal, the curtains, unusually, drawn shut. Light coming from the single fitting in the centre of the small room failed to lift the oppression of the ornate dark green wallpaper. Normally cosy and warm, courtesy of the glowing gas fire, this afternoon it felt almost tropical — on two bars, he guessed, to ensure comfort during the imminent procedure

She perched on one of the footstools, motionless, her back towards him. After a few moments, she gestured wordlessly to the plaster which sat on the adjacent table. It was much larger than he had imagined, almost the size of a tea-towel, it seemed. As he struggled to peel back the protective layer, wondering how this was going to be managed, he became aware of the tension, the silence. Clearly, the plaster was to be applied to her back, but there she was, hunched in front of him, fully clothed. Not paralysed but apparently unsure as to how to deal with the next step, maybe fearful.

To resolve the impasse, and laying the plaster face up on the table, he tentatively started to rearrange her clothing to allow him access. He was half expecting her to protest, or to push him away in a fluster of righteous objection—to insist, angrily, on getting herself ready. But after an initial stiffening of her back, she remained, rigid but uncomplaining, till he'd smoothed the plaster into place, and gently restored the layers of jumpers, cardigans. She sighed, but not, he felt, in ecstasy or even contentment. More, it seemed to him, in relief that the worst possible had not come to pass.

Over the next few months, though they became no closer, she seemed inclined to lean on him more. He still picked up the occasional Tiger loaf for her from the bakery, but now she raised more issues which appeared to require sharing whether it be her buying a new telly and deciding which model or, more importantly, the implications behind her numerous hospital appointments.

He sat with her in front of the gas fire, as they read through the letters from Dr Carnoli, her consultant at St Herbert's. They tried to figure how they squared with the conflicting pronouncements of Dr Shah, one of her GPs, whilst also wondering whether there was anything behind the beaming white-toothed smile of Dr Chindozi, who, as usual, contributed nothing. The confusion did little for her confidence, and though he shared her frustration at the incoherence, he felt that her increasingly doomy asides, the shrugging assertions that she'd likely not be around this time next year, were more a consequence of these garbled messages, than any indication of a weakening of her constitution.

Elsie, a neighbour, invited her to a sixty-fifth birthday party and, excited if only at the prospect at getting all dolled up, she'd asked him to help her get ready, and maybe to accompany her to and fro', lest she slip on the icy footpath. She chose a very fetching black dress, scattered with sequins, plunging neckline and all. Since she had nine wardrobes bursting with unworn exotica, it had probably taken a day or more to choose. She'd never lost that taste for the glamorous, the echoes of glorious nights up West.

But she hadn't lasted long at the party and, as he helped her unsteadily back home, her high-heels emphasising the slipperiness underfoot, she confided, rather dismissively, that it hadn't been what she'd call a proper party…just people standing around boozing.

No music, no dancing. She didn't touch drink, in any case, so had perched uncomfortably on the settee for a while, in front of the telly.

He helped her negotiate the stairs up to her bedroom, shoes off by now, sparkly frock back on its hanger.

Next day, on his way to the shops, he let himself in, just checking whether she needed anything, calling her name as always, so's not to catch her unawares. It was not unusual that he didn't hear her mumbled response, but he could see that the light was on in the back kitchen, and as he navigated his way through the darkened scullery, he could see her pale legs, sprawled awkwardly, across the kitchen floor.

She'd told him many times how much she'd adored Tom Jones. Not so much now though—now that he'd got old. But she did have all his records and, autograph hunting after a show at The Albert Hall, she'd actually got to kiss him…just on the cheek, though.

But when asked if she was one those who'd thrown their knickers on stage…as legend had it…a shadow, part incomprehension, part horror, had passed across her face she'd normally get to kiss him. And on the chest, though.

Wolves i: Anamnesis

M Kitton

The young boy opened his eyes to see a crack of bright light through his mismatched curtains. It was supposed to be overcast today, so they'd planned to spend the day inside watching cartoons.

But Felan wanted to go outside. He was all ready to jump on his mother to wake her, but he guessed it was still too early in the morning. He yawned as he threw his covers off and padded over to the curtains to open them. He jumped up onto the windowsill and sat down with his back against the wall, staring out at the sunrise. He watched the bright circle peek over the solid wall of trees, causing the sky around it to mutate into a variety of pinks and oranges, then glanced back into his dingy room to see it lit up without the aid of electricity. He was a curious child, and so asked a lot of questions. He had always been fascinated by science and nature, always wanting to know how things worked, and was advanced for his age. Thoughts filled his mind, and he didn't notice as the glowing ball rose higher and higher, didn't notice as it banished the darkness. He heard a soft knock on his door, turned and smiled when he saw his mother's face peaking from behind the doorframe. In the light, his mother's hair shone golden and her fawn brown eyes sparkled.

'Hey little one,' she whispered as she stepped further into the room, arms open wide. Felan leapt from his perch and flung himself at his mother.

'Mamma!' he shouted. He wrapped his arms around her neck.

She laughed, pulled him close, and kissed him on the forehead. 'Happy birthday Felan!' she said. She set him on his feet in front of her and knelt to be at his level.

'You gonna watch 'toons with me all day?' Her smile faded as she saw his face.

'Have you seen outside? It's all pretty colours!' He pouted. 'I wanna go outside! We can watch 'toons later?' he pleaded.

'Little one…you know we don't have much

money.' She stroked his cheek gently.

'I know! But I don't wanna stay inside all day! Please, Mamma…it'll be fun! We'll get ice cream at the park and see the ducks!' He bounced on the spot in poorly contained excitement.

'Okay Felan, let's get changed first, yeah? Then we'll head out. Sound good?' She grinned as he ran over to his shoes to pull them on.

'Yes! I'll wait here Mamma!' he shouted as he shoved his feet into his favourite (and only) pair of black shoes.

His mother lingered by the door and turned back round to face her son, his eyes lit up at such a simple thing. This was special for him, as he never really got to go outside. It was quite sad that such a small idea was the cause for all his excitement. She left the room, went into her shared room and got dressed. It wasn't much, but she swore to make this day his best birthday ever.

The water rippled in the slight breeze. The warm air tousled Felan's and ruffled his mother's blonde hair as they stood on the bank. The layers of blue got deeper and darker, much to Felan's fascination. Mother and son sat hand in hand, as they ate their ice cream on the old park bench under the trees. The sun above them had scorched the grass at their feet, some invisible force wearing away the patches since the last time they'd been there. The child asked his mother an endless stream of nonsense questions. His mother chuckled as he managed to get the ice cream on the end of his nose but protested as he smeared it over her face. She started to tickle him the second he'd finished eating, his laughter coming out in raspy gasps and squeals. Her face flushed a deep shade of red, as she relented and let him escape her spindly fingers. He tackled her to the ground, digging deep into her sides or faintly brushing his fingers over any exposed skin as her shirt rode up revealing a patch of tanned skin.

The walk back home was easy going. The mother tightened her grip on the boy's hand and ran a hand through his hair.

'Did you have fun today little one?'

'It was awesome Mamma!' He grinned. 'Did you see how long I had you down?' He finished happily, bouncing in his step. A frown crossed his face. 'I just wished that daddy wasn't working. He would've had fun with us.'

His mother's smile faded, and when he looked at her in concern (too much for a seven-year-old) she replied, 'he's trying to get more money, so he can buy you that toy you've wanted for ages.'

Felan nodded. 'It's been the best day today Mamma. I love you.' His eyes lit up as the grin returned to her face.

'I love you too little one,' she replied, bending down to kiss him on the cheek.

She didn't see the car.

As she stood back up, they were already in its path as it barrelled down the sidewalk. She wrenched her hand free from her son's, picked him up, and tossed him to the side of the road. A second later, the car sent her body sailing down the road.

Felan sat up, confused as to why his mother had thrown him onto the grass. He looked to where he had last seen her, but all that remained was a faint trail of exhaust fumes and as he glanced after them, the car from which they came was already out of sight. He stood up on weak legs, eyes roaming the scene before him. He could hear screams and frenzied shouts…and he was baffled. His mother had been right beside him. He saw a body spread-eagled on the floor, long blonde hair covering the front of her face…

'Mamma!' He screamed as he ran over to her, his little legs pumping.

As he reached her a pair of arms caught him around his waist and pulled him back.

'Stay here kid. You don't want to see that,' a deep

voice said.

'Mamma!' He screamed again, a single tear rolling down his cheek. He thrashed in the strange man's grip. 'Mamma wake up! Please, Mamma!' He wailed and sank to his knees; the man's vice-like grip restrained him. Felan heard sirens in the distance, and he turned his head to watch the arrival of the flashing blue lights. The vehicles emitted multiple people dressed in yellow.

Blood started flowing from beneath her head, stained her blonde hair. The air turned cold, and the breeze that swept through was no longer comforting. As the paramedics reached his mother, the strong arms spun Felan around one hundred and eighty degrees to shield him from the scene.

'Mamma...No...Mamma!' he cried as he tried to fight the arms. A soft hand touched his tear stained cheek and he stopped resisting enough to stare up at the man in front of him.

The man sported shorts and a beige t-shirt. He had straight, cropped red hair. 'My name's Tristan, kid. What's yours?'

'F..Felan...and I'm not supposed to talk to strangers.' He sniffled.

The man nodded. 'That's a very smart thing to do. Hey, do you want to ride in the back of the car?'

He flagged down one of the paramedics. Felan

stood up, wiped his face and grasped Tristan's hand tightly. They walked over to the paramedic car that had arrived within seconds of the ambulance and got into the back seat together. The woman driver looked at the boy.

Felan drowsed, his face buried in Tristan's chest as his breathing evened out.

'I'm so sorry Felan,' he whispered.

'Was she your wife sir?' the woman said as she watched the two through the rear-view mirror.

Tristan shook his head. 'No...I don't know them.'

The car sped off after the ambulance.

'It's my birthday,' Felan mumbled.

Fingers

G Frosh

Nobody used the back gate but him. For them, it led nowhere of interest and was a negligible place to be. But for him, it was a haven—dark there, and sunken…almost hidden. And there was the air-raid shelter, where he could do and be all those things that were forbidden, or at least frowned upon, which was almost worse.

Maybe one day he'd have a bicycle. It would live in that place—would have to be concealed in that way, because a bike was forbidden. He was the only one. M went to school on his as a matter of course, and other kids also were allowed. But somehow, he was made an exception. The air-raid shelter, dripping but friendly, waiting to be of service once more.

The family, somewhat strangely, were apart. It was by choice. Maybe because, in some way, they felt they were indeed The Chosen. His friends from school were not exactly welcomed at the house where he lived, but, almost grudgingly, were allowed, because, even so, a child needs some friends, albeit unsuitable ones.

So that summer he was not reluctant to do some work for Dad. It took him away from a particular sense of solitude, but also proved a source of new and exciting visions, to be stored amongst the fantasies by which he was sustained. And when it was getting near school time again, his work almost done, he was surprised and thrilled to be rewarded, not with passing approval of his efforts but, unexpectedly, with a large white and crisp five-pound note — its size and purity seeming like exceptional recognition, not just of his labour, but of his very existence.

The possibilities were overwhelming. But it would be too much, bound to be met with the most adamant rebuff. He knew that a bike would be out of the question; and worse, there was the fear of the row, and the guilt he'd be made to feel — how he'd let them down. He wrestled and squirmed, trying to sidestep the obvious, but there was no way round it.

He must get a bike, but somehow not a bike.

No-one in his family made things, but during the summer of work, there had been Harry the blacksmith and Jim the mechanic and Ted the driver. All could turn their hands to stuff. He was inspired. It was possible.

Out of the back gate, across the road, another world was there. Not the people so much.

Somehow, they didn't exist for him. More the shape of the land. Before the flats had been built, the thumping pile-drivers cracking glass in Dad's fish tank, the far pavement marked the edge of a very steep cliff. From there, no doubt, in the distance and far below, you could have seen the broad river. But now, from down in the hollow, the tall blocks of the new Lansbury Estate rose to meet you and, giving little recognition to ground level, continued upwards, floor on floor, as high again, looming.

If you wanted to enter that world, to arrive down there, it meant tramping the path. It was a long way down and the path was a steep black ribbon. No-one seemed to use it. It was ideal.

On the morning, and with Johnny Mathews' help, he trundled his contraption across the zebra and along to the top of the path. He was proud of what he had made.

It was well put together, the pram wheels spun sweetly, and the steering seemed to work just fine…a tug on the rope, this way or that, would send him wherever he wanted to go.

Aware of the steepness of the path, he'd paid special attention to the brakes, ensuring that the stout wooden lever would bear strongly on the back wheels. That would surely slow him down if things got hairy.

The path was clear as usual, and, confident in his machine, he was eager for the thrill.

But more so, it was the chance to show that he too could be trusted. Maybe not out on the road, as yet, but surely…after this, there could be no doubt.

A push from Johnny, with a yell of encouragement, and he was off down the path. The machine felt driven, and as the speed built it responded perfectly to every input on the steering. Halfway down and for an instant, it felt, of course, as if he were flying. He'd never been so fast, even in Ted's van, and that could go some. The black path had seemed so smooth from up high, but not at this speed, spectacles jolting on his nose as he bounced across the broken surface. Almost immediately, eyes began to stream. His breath was held, teeth clamped, but, in exhilaration, he sensed the making of a triumph. He'd shown them!

Nearing the bottom, and at full speed, it was time to slow down, the path swooping round a gentle curve towards the entrance of the nearest block. He reached behind to apply the brakes, not wanting any mishap to spoil the perfection of his record-breaking run.

He missed the wooden lever, and his hand came in contact with the spokes of the back wheel. The skin was flayed off all the fingers, there was blood everywhere.

I've never owned a bicycle.

The Orchard

O Goodall

The garden was large and green, bushy and very isolated. To the sides, orchards stretched down the hill, apples hanging heavy from spindly limbs. The garden and the house were a good ten minutes' drive from town. Martin and Christopher made their own apple juice and were happy with this.

Martin held a senior position in a well-respected newspaper and was having some time off from a particularly hectic schedule. Christopher was a writer and had had a novel published early of that year. It had been fairly well received, critically at least, and he was hoping to have even greater success with his current work-in-progress, though that progress had halted of late.

They often took breakfast together, making the most of the weather and of course of being able to enjoy the apple juice — from the garden — in the garden itself.

They were having breakfast outside one morning when the man walked calmly out from the bushes towards them. Gentle in his movements. Placid eyes.

As he approached, the two seated men became uncomfortable in their chairs. Momentarily they looked all at one another. The man looked vaguely Arabic and indeed had a slight accent.

'May I please have a shot of apple juice please?'

Martin half-opened his mouth and glanced over to Christopher, whose alert eyes he caught flickeringly before he answered.

'Err, well, err, I don't know. Yes, I suppose so. Yes, I suppose you can, yes certainly. I don't see why not, do you, Chris?'

'I don't see why not.'

Haltingly, unsure of his movements and of how to treat this man, Martin poured him a small glass of juice.

'There, here you go!'

Martin still standing, Christopher still seated, the golden liquid swilled and shone in the glass as the man swung it up to his mouth and gulped it down, his bright eyes savouring its sweetness. He paused a little too long after he drank, then placed the glass firmly but carefully upon the table. A soft clink.

'Thank you. Very nice. Thank you very much.'

He turned and disappeared beyond the bushes.

He returned the next day and the scene was repeated. And the next. He was perfectly pleasant, perfectly civil, and neither of them could see any problem with his coming each morning. They began to wonder if they should perhaps offer him something more if he came again.

He did. Came with his measured walk, his dirtied shoes softly brushing the grass. Martin and Christopher were silent as he approached, waiting for him to be at a reasonable distance to speak to him.

'May I please join you for breakfast please?'

Christopher's question caught in his throat and Martin could not quite speak for a second either.

'Yes of course. In fact, we were just thinking of asking just that ourselves.'

He sat, and he joined them for breakfast. Christopher prepared an egg sandwich for him and Martin supplied him with an apple juice. He did not say much, nor indeed did any of them, but the atmosphere was pleasant, and they relaxed into a brief conversation on how they made the apple juice before lapsing into an almost assured silence.

He returned the next day too, rejecting their offer of food but accepting the apple juice. They wondered if they had perhaps done something to upset him, something wrong. The following day when he arrived he accepted both breakfast and juice. The same almost assured silence returned to the table. Not a lack of noise, but peaceful.

'May I please stay with you please? I have nowhere to live and nowhere to go.'

Christopher's confusion was palpable. Martin's mouth hung open more visibly, but only momentarily.

'Err, I'm not really sure we'd be able to do that. Maybe.'

'Indeed, I don't know how good an idea that would be.'

'Don't know really. It'd be something we'd have to think about.'

The silence returned, remained. But less peaceful this time. A pointed silence, lacking conversation. The man remained perfectly civil to them. They to him. They finished breakfast. He set his glass firmly but carefully upon the table. A gentle clink.

'Thank you. Very nice. Thank you very much.'

He nodded and turned and disappeared beyond the bushes.

He returned the following morning and when he did, Martin and Christopher quickly offered him the apple juice and egg sandwich. They sat and ate. There was a tight silence in the air, even when they spoke. They could not cover it up. The man broke it finally.

'Would it be possible to stay? I have nowhere to stay.'

'Well we've thought about it, but it wouldn't really work so well. Or that's what it seems, as there's just not that much space.'

'And with work. That makes things difficult.'

'But we thought maybe you could stay the night this evening.'

'Yes, you can stay the night this evening, if you want?'

'Thank you.' He nodded.

They looked after him meticulously. Almost anything he needed or wanted either Martin or Christopher made sure he got. Late that night they made him a bed from the sofa and armchair cushions, arranging them carefully in the middle of the living room floor, with blankets and a pillow.

When they came downstairs the next morning they found he had risen early and set the breakfast table, everything ready and waiting for them. They ate and after they all had finished he set about — despite their protests — clearing the table and washing the breakfast things.

'Thank you. Very nice. Thank you very much. Farewell.'

A nod.

He did not come the next day, or the next. Nor for the rest of the week.

That weekend, Christopher sat in the armchair in the living room, reading the supplement of the newspaper. He was skimming a story about a man shot dead by a local farmer — now in custody — for trespassing. The victim was identified as Aref Basha-Qabbani, a Syrian. Apparently, he had been sleeping in one of the barns. But what caught Christopher's eye was the photo. He realised they had never asked his name. Slowly he crumpled the newspaper shut, rested it softly on his lap and stared ahead, at the wall opening in front of him.

As the Day Ends

K Coombs

As the day ends, she climbs into bed. 'One last day,' she whispers. She closes her eyes and then she falls asleep.

He's trapped! With nowhere to run and no one to ask for help! He feels the four walls around him closing in, suffocating from the lack of oxygen. He bangs on the walls and screams out, hoping someone can hear him but there's no one around.

She wakes up with a massive smile on her face. Today is the day her life finally changes! She jumps out of bed and starts to get washed and dressed, it's gonna be a long day but she is more than ready.

His breathing fastens, panicking that he will never escape. Stuck in this box, stuck in his own mind, he's going to go insane. If only someone would have taken him seriously. If only someone would have listened.

Now she's washed and dressed, it's time for some breakfast. Toast? Fruit? Bacon and eggs? She really can't decide! Bacon and eggs, it is! As she takes a bite, she thinks about what she has to do today, and she goes over the checklist saved in her mind.

Kicking and screaming surely someone must hear him? His voice is growing hoarse and it's starting to hurt! Water! He needs water but there's nothing with him, he's all alone.

Breakfast finished, she heads upstairs and grabs the bag she packed last night. Her friends were off on holiday in Spain, but this trip was going to be so much better. She takes a look around the room she grew up in, 'this is gonna feel so weird coming back here' she thought and then she shut the door and left.

He could hear someone, maybe a crowd. There was hope after all! He screamed again! Using every bit of strength to kick and punch his way out, they've heard him! He can finally get out of here!

She arrived at her destination, only a few hours' drive but the nerves were starting to kick in. She wasn't doubting the trip, she was finally realising this moment was here! She got out of the car, hugged her parents goodbye and off she went.

He could hear the sledgehammers breaking down the walls around him. 'Not long now,' he thought.

She laid down in bed. 'This is It,' she repeated over and over in her head. The trip of the century, the one she had been patiently waiting for! Her phone pinged, a message from the girls! 'Good luck today babe! #WishYouWereHere.' Attached was a photo of them all sipping a cocktail in the sun...she knew she'd rather be alone on this trip then be with them on theirs.

'Hang on in there mate. We'll be with you shortly! Not long until you'll be sipping a nice cold beer in the sun! We're breaking you out as quickly as we can.'

I have no idea who he is but thank god he heard me! It feels like I've been here for decades!

Her eyes opened, drowsy from all of the meds, she pulled off the oxygen mask and reached for the glass of water in front of her.

'Ouch!' She winced in pain!

'I'll grab that for you,' the doctor said sweetly.

The lid was coming off, I could see the sunlight shining through! Any second now I'd be able to escape this box, I'll be able to breathe! I saw the room around me, I saw the bright lights.

She looked at the doctor and waited for him to talk…

'Mr Parker, the operation was a success. You're going to be in a lot of pain for a while, but you'll heal nicely over time. Take it easy and no reaching for water okay?' He joked.

'So, is that it now? No more surgeries, no more appointments, no more he/she jokes?'

'I can't make a promise about the jokes, but I can say that you are now officially finished with the reassignment and you can now experience a life where you physically and mentally match. You've been extremely brave with what you've done. You should be proud of yourself for being who you should be.'

'I guess that means I'm free, I'm not trapped, I'm no longer suffocating! Thank you so much, Doctor! I don't think I'll ever be able to repay you for the gift you've just given me'

'There is no need to thank me, Mr Parker, it is my job! I'm just sorry you had to miss the holiday to Spain with your friends'

'After years of feeling like I was buried alive, I know I'm exactly where I'm supposed to be!'

Sawtooth Waves

S A Finlay

George was halfway through a battery of pre-op tests in the hospital—but they called it The Menders these days. He was nervous, felt it in the high-speed invisible twitch of his right eye. The tests were nothing to do with his heart. For some reason, everyone seemed more bothered about his head.

'When do we get on to my heart?' he'd said, in that diffident gangly way of his, staring at the nurse with the bedside manner, as his head was locked into a white plastic basket. His huge feet stuck out over the end of the tunnel. Did that matter?

'There there, pet,' said the kindly nurse, towering over him, like a mannequin come to life, who'd learnt to smile and hug and reassure. She patted his hands. She was quite the Miss Bedside Manner.

She had warm hands. He couldn't see the perfect half-moons of her nails. Every man, he reckoned, wanted to be touched by warm hands — whatever his orientation. That was the point. Back in the day, didn't someone say, 'warm hands, cold heart?' Or was it the other way round?

'We do want to check your sawtooth waves. No point in a new heart if your mind can't cope. And there's a lot of twitching going on with that lovely brown eye and that lovely green eye of yours.'

'I've twitched forever and a day. I just do, when I'm nervous, but nobody notices it except me,' said George. 'Normally,' he added.

He was trying to remonstrate, to be reasonable, convincing. A Master Clinical Psychologist had told him he had a natural if clumsily born gravitas about him, was trustworthy and charismatic, possessed all the traits that promised a career trajectory following a straightforward exponential curve, were he to be *simply. faintly. more. assertive.* A made man. Before his heart was broken and things flattened a bit.

'Aren't I here for the sake of my heart?' he said — assertively — through the plastic muntin things, quite a feat of mind over matter, he reckoned. He tried to look about him. Impossible. He looked up at her blue eyes, the halo of dark hair, the blue-white of the room. He wanted to go back to Waiting Room One.

Waiting Room One was an anthem to the comfort of scruffy antiquity, all dark old-fashioned rugs, leather pouffes, proper books that smelt of something — a stamp of authority and wisdom and thoughtfulness, sparkling elucidating or haunting prose on real woodworm-less shelves, polished wood cabinets, decanters promising rare uncontaminated liquids — water probably. Not a screen in site. It had been like walking onto the set of one of those costume dramas that used to be popular before Nostalgia was decreed as inefficient as Social Media Gushing. A new tried and tested sedative: a recycling of elements of a bad past for extenuating circumstances. Or some such. He'd admired the design and execution.

'Yes, but mind and body both. Trust us. We know our stuff,' said the MBM. She had a nice voice. The voice of a mother. 'The first new hearts failed. Pointless. Painful. Expensive. That's the PPE paradigm we all learnt. The neurologists caught up: the algorithms speak to us. Symbiotic, you see. But of course,' she said, patting him again, 'you know this. So now, we cannot mend your broken heart, unless we take a looksie in your head.' She leaned over close to the white basket and eye-balled him as if she were flirting with him. He remembered flirting. Those were the days, when you could look sideways, lean in, graze the hand or arm, take a face in your cupped hands, adjust a stray hair, or, more like, pull a self-conscious face and blush and accidentally rub shoulder to shoulder as you guffawed, without getting marched off to some Relationship Therapy Classes for Men

'I suppose so,' he said. 'I can cope with my head, though. I just can't bear the pain in my heart anymore.'

'Nobody has to simply *cope*. You know we got better than that. For people like you anyway. You're pretty Alpha, after all. You're tremendously lucky. And of course, worthy. The system suggests you are.'

'Bloody system. Google says I am? Or Amazon? Or Unified Banking does? Or Facebook? I don't use Facebook. I feel worthless. And my heart is broken as a result. Or vice versa, depending on your logic,' he said. He sounded a bit hollow. He knew that. It was inevitable — what with the wrecked heart and his head locked in the way it was.

'Tut tut! We don't mind a bit of heresy with nerves,' she laughed. 'Mind you, take care. Three strikes and you go in the Beta queue. Ooh, how can you not use Facebook? Facebook uses *you*, actually. Excuse the delay. I'm waiting for the blasted green light. Been a few glitches.'

'That's not very confidence-inspiring. Can I have my head out of the basket?'

74

'Once you've said you're in, you're in! Though I like your sense of humour. There's bits of the throwback about you,' she said in a tinny voice.

He could hear her tapping her feet. He couldn't remember if she was wearing heels. He liked to imagine that she was. He remembered heels before they were outlawed for all but the few. Made a woman stand…the right way. Of course, what any woman wore and how any woman looked, was of little consequence to him. Only the one woman. And she'd been a bit practical for the most part. And all that, of course, was why he was here.

'The odd power-fail,' she said apologetically. Then she added, 'Have you seen my latest pictures?'

'I don't go there. Camera fibs,' he said, by way of explanation, then added, 'not about you, I didn't mean that. You're very perfect. Just, I've been let down before with it.'

'Ah, yes. But dating at your age. With a broken heart. A contradiction. Hopefully, we'll resolve this for you, when we mend your heart. Oops, got the green light.'

'I'm only seventy-five!' he protested as he slid into the tunnel.

Whatever the sawfish waves were, and why his right eye twitched invisibly, were irrelevant in the context of his other metrics—which bespoke a healthy enough mind—and he was fast-tracked to the heart-replacers. Two months! He had two months to wait: There must be quite a backlog of broken hearts. Amongst the Alphas. For all he knew, everyone right through to the poor Omegas drifted about under the thumping ballast of them. He didn't want to think about this. He went about his everyday life. He waited.

His everyday life mostly consisted of thinking about his broken heart. About Sally. George liked to walk. He ambled like a sprightly carefree young man. He was lithe and fit at his age, he had undyed hair of a pleasant silver sheen, no craggy jowls, neat eyebrows. He dressed anonymously in that stylish charcoal grey of the affluent and wise. Outwardly he seemed mature, confident, approachable, dignified: nobody would conjecture that his smart shirt concealed some catastrophic failure to simply be. He lived in the City. He didn't like transport: everything was driverless. Back in his day, someone took responsibility, took the wheel. He avoided trains— they made him feel like he was being hurtled at high speed towards an unknown invisible wall—you couldn't see what lay ahead in them. What you can't see can hurt you, he reasoned. As for planes, before, you could see the clouds, which was bad enough, but you could be poetic with your fear: 'Here I am, with my head in the clouds!' Now, some robotic traffic controller could get artificially pissed off; the plane would cease its hermetically sealed progression across the skies in a whimsical nanosecond, a twitch of your overactive eye muscles, and down you hurtled as you tried to communicate your imminent demise in your allotted screen panic-time. Ships: ploughing across the oceans, bumping into each other — so much went by water, understandably, congestion had clogged up the waves. And the law-courts. Rockets were fine, because they…well, rocketed, backed up by a lot of power, and shot off to where they were going, mostly just a nice little day's orbit to take in the view. He'd turned one of those rewards down recently. But at least rockets went so PDQ you couldn't overthink your neuroses. He also avoided the countryside. He found vast green spaces and beautiful impressionist views: angry inky skies, sweeping curved cliffs, buckets of lakes and gradients of hills and mountains, ancient architecture, and the chirruping of nature, tedious. What wasn't human irritated him. (Sally had been a bit of an eco-warrior. He'd gone along with it. They once went to Iceland. On a plane. A gesture of unconditional love on his part. A cold slippery expensive caper. He quite enjoyed it. All white and clean, with occasional outraged geysers surprising the terrain and him out of his languor and disaffection—a hot and bothered ambush of frozen tranquillity.) He walked. Didn't matter if it rained. Or snowed. He dictated emails, tweeted, posted, sent messages, drafted reports, as he paced the pavements. To passers-by, he might look like a lonely person, chittering to himself. George didn't give a damn if he looked like a forgotten lunatic. Truly, that was what he felt like anyway. He wasn't the type to pretend to be other than he was. Besides, the rest of the walkers were doing exactly the same thing, conversing with something disembodied a few metres ahead of them. For all he knew, they were doing what the world did these days, pretending to be busy and popular at the same time. At least texting with your thumbs and fingers in transit had been banned. He remembered a bad spate of accidents. He was working for a smartphone marketing company then. Share prices tumbled and so did he…nearly. He was in demand because he was good, good at persuading people they wanted stuff, campaigning, researching markets. So, he went and marketed drones after that. They'd had a bad rap for a while when Amazon dropped a government payload (never disclosed) in someone's back garden on the wrong child's head. This wasn't any old kid.

This was some big-shot Alpha's kid. But he rebooted the market. Drones were clever, light, a bit like Da Vinci might have imagined, centuries ago. Aesthetically and practically they made sense.

George was always gainfully employed, unlike the Unemployed, who VR-gamed all day in their ghettos. Everyone wanted George. He excelled at his job. Especially in March. It was good to be busy, needed, even if you rarely met those that needed you in person. When you'd finished being busy, you could return to the basement of your block and work out in the gym, nod at everyone else sweating and rowing or running, then ascend in the lift to your sterile pristine apartment and put your music on and prepare yourself a nice meal and stream something compelling, then, rarely, read before falling asleep. And getting up again to do the same. It was good, this activity. The only way to accommodate the thoughts of the broken heart. Only, you knew you had to do something about it: you couldn't keep bad company forever. Unlike most, George refused to date. Swipe right or left. (He'd tried all that once. A disaster.) Or ask his AI assistant to calculate and suggest and organise. Even hover in a bar. Be passively introduced. Nope. Sally had to go first. She'd taken up residence. She was a sitting tenant in any one of his four chambers. He never quite knew where she was squatting. She had to be forcibly evicted so that he could go on. Putting one foot in front of the other. On pavements.

Still, it was set to be a long two months. There was no holiday from the heart. It ached. He could hear it in the dark, feel its work in the pulse. He'd taken to comporting himself aristocratically, one hand tucked inside his jacket, fingertips connecting with it, tapping a Morse code, 'are you there? I know you're there. Not for long. It's got to stop. Sally. I mean you. Not my heart! Enough's enough. A man has to live.' As he walked about. He determined to see no one, work, adhere to an ascetic routine for the whole two months. At lunchtimes, he'd promenade about and…happen upon The Menders. He'd pass by Waterloo station and out and around and…arrive and stare up at it. He'd ignore the crowds. 'Me soon,' he'd mutter to nobody in particular. Himself. 'After that, I'll be ok,' and he'd whistle. And people would stare, at the odd expression he pulled…whistling, eyes blinking rapidly.

He was back at the Menders soon enough. He was in the Choices Room. Everything about it was silly — sure he was partly responsible for this, although he comforted himself that he was simply a baton carrier or standard-bearer, that he hadn't started the whole mind-boggling infinite warehouse, neither had he, personally, invented the notion of making people know what they wanted before they knew that they wanted it. Genius marketing, keeping perfectly ordinary nice people coveting, tapping into cupidity. Or stupidity. George knew he was kind and was good at what he did and had a conscience about it, and after all, he had a broken heart, so he felt he was decent to a degree. Still, he remembered when it wasn't like this, when you mended and made do and got on with stuff. It was just that he was tired, and he might go on a bit too long, and really, Sally had to be jettisoned. Lock stock and barrel, the container ship with her, the whole thing demolished. But it was ridiculous. How many mechanical-organic-hearts *were* there? He knew his stuff. He knew *they* knew what would fit and that things would work. Sure, here he was, privileged, oh yes, privileged to be living now, with endless possibilities! It was a marvel. He must just get on and deal with the candy-flossed décor and try not to smirk at the inane swiping and scrolling next to him. He sat there as long as he could bear it. He chose his heart. *I choose thee! Out damned Sally! No? Then I'll dismantle and replace your shelter, I want to love again!* He made it abundantly clear that they'd already chosen it for him, that he knew the infinite options were in fact actually limited, that his immaculate manners prevented him from simply saying *no!* to the ridiculous cabaret of the Choices Room, that he was a very bad performer, and that he'd now sat there swiping and scrolling and feigning interest for longer than his natural sincerity or lack of poker face would allow. He was ready to get on with it. It was a dreadful phoney sort of foreplay—you were supposed to get excited at the prospect of your rib-cage being broken and getting carved down the middle and, then...he supposed one heart kept pumping while the other was revved into action and then there'd be this moment of switching on and off, some calibration lasting fractional seconds between the one pump and the other. A handover. A takeover bid more like. This whole charade was supposed to stop you thinking about the goriness of it, about how your life hung by that thread: trust in the system. His problem was he overthought. He contemplated the mud of a distant childhood when there was some difference between town and country. He imagined running through barley fields and hearing bees and gusts of breeze. And pubs with open fires. It was nice. It surprised him that something he professed to loathe was so comforting and attractive. Not like the concrete and candyfloss and primped parks of the unbounded city he insisted he preferred.

He was halfway into these disaffected topsy-turvy thoughts when a sweet girl shuffled in. She seemed as nonplussed and abstracted as he was. Confused by the room. He saw a couple of fellow mendees raise their heads and make as if to hiss at her. Poor dear thing. She stood — oddly. He cocked his head, staring sideways, smiled one of his kindly smiles, managed to glance at her feet. Ah yes. Very strange indeed. He'd never seen the like. Mind you, she'd probably never seen the likes of the sitting tenant in his four chambers. He got up and left the room and headed for Waiting Room Two. She'd be there, he assumed, soon enough.

He was wearing a plastic baby wraparound. Feeling self-conscious. This waiting room screamed its high tech-ness, its cleverness, its advancement. Fear of clinical white was nonsense once you were on the up — diagnosed and ready for messing about with. You only needed all that reassuring stuffy antique shit of Waiting Room One when you were wondering what could be done about yourself, and if the science had arrived, and been put to use. Once you got the green light, it was all about calm tranquil unconscious blank clean sterile white and silver. He approved. He thought he did. He really wanted to talk to someone. That'd be nice.

The lovely young woman sidled like a crab in a bubble-wrap race. She had dark eyes, asymmetrical in some way, that he couldn't quite establish the detail of, a polished face with a mournful expression on it. She shambled to a halt next to him and levered herself into a reclining chair after some tried and tested fashion that he'd noticed earlier. He leaned over as if to say, 'let me,' but she shook her head dumbly. He sat there for a while, wondering if it was ok to talk.

'So,' he said, 'what are you in for?'

She stared at him.

'I didn't mean to be rude. I'm George. I'm getting a new heart! Fancy that! My head's ok though. I won't be heartbroken anymore!'

She raised her eyebrows, squinted carefully at him, then pointed at her ears. Her ears. Like two pet symmetrical question marks about her lovely face.

'Oh! I'm sorry! You're deaf? You're getting those mended?' George was confused. He thought it was the foot, that's what his earlier observation had suggested. Why would someone put their foot over their ears?

She raised her shoulders and eyebrows in a massive confused shrug. She pointed at her feet.

'Your feet?' It was definitely to do with the feet. He hadn't been wrong.

She shook her head. Pointed at *one* foot.

He bent down. Peered carefully. He could see the foot, or what appeared to be a foot. It looked the wrong shape. It was doing its best to break free from its plastic.

'Ah!' he said, 'Your foot! It looks like an interesting foot! No shoes eh?' He smiled at her, a look of understanding of something, about women and shoes perhaps, across his face. 'Rather your foot than your ears?'

She shook her head again, this time furiously, seemed in turns angry, sad, distressed, uncertain. Finally, she started singing. An extraordinary song he'd never heard before, and he'd listened to enough music. A serenade? About a man who had a perfect woman? About a man who wanted a perfect woman? About a woman who would be perfect for a man? But it was a song to tug at strings, break your heart (George didn't need that—he was feeling pretty fragile as it was in those matters) and he drew back. It was curious, a song of love, of the future, and a song of farewell, all rolled into one: upbeat and fast, then elegiac refrains. He didn't know whether he wanted to laugh or cry. A sort of hip-hop swansong. Bach gone a bit far or Schubert getting rather cheerful occasionally. He couldn't quite decide what it was.

Neither could he fathom how she could sing like that if she were deaf.

They were both silent. The waiting room took on an air of doubt and ambivalence. Shadows slunk across it from nowhere. It fell dark suddenly.

'Oops, another little glitch. My oh my! We're getting a few of those. Grid's overloaded with Alphas. Betas on the way up, more like!' said a cheerful voice that sounded like MBM. 'I'll double-check the system priorities. Don't want either of you going whoopsie on the table, now do we? I'll extend the dark time first. Reboot. It'll be peaceful for you both. Don't sing too much Ebony, or you'll put a strain on your energy reserves. There's a pet.'

'Ebony? That's your name?' said George.

He saw her head, curiously nodding in the dark.

'That's nice. All will be well. This is guaranteed. You're so very young. I suppose that voice is your fortune?' He perceived that she shrugged again. It wouldn't do to pry, but the doleful fact was you needed a lot of money to get any Alpha treatment. He had more than he needed, and he reckoned he had that simply because he'd been born in the right decade. In fact, this op was horrifically expensive, he had nothing to spend his modest funds on except his unrequited love, and giving your money away was pretty much banned after the swingeing tax rises that were supposed to *take care of everything*. That voice of hers was ineffably something else and it was fair enough to speculate that even if she hadn't made a fortune because someone would have Svengali-ed his way into making more than her share out of her, still, here she was, and she had enough. And what sane person wouldn't want to walk tall and confidently in shoes? For God's sake, he'd seen some disabilities in his time, he'd done his bit to help, but… a webbed foot, that had to get a person down.

She hummed for a bit. The lights came on. They came for her first. They were kind. MBM was extravagantly attentive, extending those warm hands of hers, gently swivelling her, aiding her, walking her towards a door on the left.

He got up and grabbed her hand. MBM frowned. He ignored her. He clutched Ebony's hand.

'It's been so very nice to meet you. You're quite extraordinary. I'll see you after, maybe? Always sing like that, and the world over will love you. The world over must *surely* love you as you are!' he spluttered.

Good grief! Had he just made a declaration of love? Was Sally nudging him? He placed his other hand on his ailing heart, tap, tap tapped it. *Are you there?* he was asking her in his perfectly sound head (he knew he was sound of mind because they'd told him the sawtooth waves were nothing out of the ordinary, after all). He couldn't hear Sally bumping about in his four chambers. Maybe she was hiding. Normally, he could feel she was there, echoes, reverberations, rumblings. He just couldn't make her out. She was canny, that was for sure, but this was evasiveness of a high order.

MBM was getting impatient. She tapped her heels. Yes, she was wearing heels, just as he'd imagined, lovely shoes. Ebony stared at the shoes, deprivation in her eyes. How strange—George saw that one eye was eyelash-less. MBM's warm left hand pressed down on Ebony's shoulder, so that Ebony was in a sort of vice, couldn't look other than straight ahead. MBM's right hand went up, ten centimetres from George's nose. Like one of those old great big policed or lollipop-manned *Stop!* sign. Right in his face.

'Look,' she said, an inscrutable smile on her flawless face. She hissed: 'She's a *Beta!* Married up. The voice *got* her here. Queue-jumped. And the husband wants the foot. He *owns* the bloody foot *and* the bloody voice. And she's off to get that foot sorted. *Now!* So, no more of your beautiful protestations George? There's a pet. And I'm on the clock here. And let's remember, those little hammerings in your interior—we're getting that sorted for you so that you don't over-emote, and you can have a long and contented life and get partnered up again.

Remember? Yes, you do. Good handsome boy. So, let go of the poor creature's hand. And I'll be back for you in a jiffy.'

'Good grief!' said George, stunned as equally by the novelty of MBM's surging outrage and fugitive manners as by the information about the sweet web-footed girl.

'Oh, for fuck's sake, George, dear. She can't hear. I'm really going to have to go and have a session in the Relaxation Suite if you try my patience any longer. You're breaking rules! Which will mean another twenty minutes wait for you if you're not careful. Am I being clear?'

'Perfectly,' said George. He let go of Ebony. Ebony felt him let go. She dropped her head sideways, some sort of valediction to him. Their joint doubts now dissected by the gorgeous nurse with the fleeing bedside manners.

He sat down. He watched them go…through the door on the right… a no-turning-back sort of a door, a no-holds-barred portal to who you wanted to be, who you imagined you wanted to be. Uncertainty seized him. His chest hurt. He tapped it. Was she there? *Sally, are you there? Knock knock!* He couldn't find her. *Are you having a power nap?* Where the heck was she? If she wasn't there, what did that mean?

Had she done a bunk, surrendered? What about the girl? That voice?

'I'm overthinking,' he said. He closed his eyes and waited the remaining ten minutes. He could feel his eyelids fluttering like billy-o. Sawtooth waves.

'Your turn!' hollered the nurse, standing over him suddenly, smiling once more, the warm hands reaching for him.

I remember her sigh

R Golden

Go to London or some city. Feel lost. Someone's died. Life's empty. She arranged all our life outside of work. Social life, friends…they were all hers. No one to share life with. No one to speak with, to listen to, no one to touch. Her warm skin, her warm lips. Her beauty. Void

So, to that city. Wandering, alone. Left on my own. Well, not left, not abandoned but snared by reality— the material of her body gave way. Surprised, unexpected. Unbelievable.

The city's not as it used to be. Where's the drama, the sparkle, the hidden secrets to discover, the concert hall as the band played on, the art gallery with the glistening oils, the friends, her friends with the humour and monologues, dialogues? Hers. I knew I was accepted as in 'tolerated'. But I was pleased. She spoke with passion, clarity and always joy. They listened. I watched.

Nothing recognisable. Maybe it's the wrong city. Maybe the train brought me to the wrong station. Maybe I just can't remember. Often, she said my memory was poor. Gaps, sudden black spots. I couldn't always call up the title cards as I used to. I couldn't fill the names in as if the projector in my brain had dimmed.

The streets glisten. Cobble's glisten. Cobblestones? I've no recollection of cobblestones in this city, our city. Shops look vaguely familiar. Selling clothes, screwdrivers, trombones, tombstones, a camera, cigarettes and oranges.

A restaurant is what I need. A place to assemble, to marshal thoughts, memories, fragments like glueing together a torn photo. This one's too posh, that one's too meaty, there a bad odour, here just cakes and that one is too commercial — a crap chain, but this one, 'organic' it says, seasonal. Looks okay. Bet they won't use garlic though.

We used to live off garlic. An elixir we thought would sustain us forever. But not her. She was not sustained. An insult to our lives. To our abstinence. Did I say her liver packed up? What a shock. What pain. I lived her pain. Yes, I do feel poorly now. Just a hangover. I probably need more garlic.

I say 'need more' but what nonsense. It's how we live…I embody my civilisation, the civilisation that doesn't work…there's the wars, the medications, the diets, so what do we do? We throw more of the same at it. We have shock and awe, surges, stronger insecticides, more tablets, less garlic. Nonsense. We own nonsense as we own our march into oblivion.

There's something uncomfortable here. An odour of cleaning fluid, distant toilets, dog fur…something. I've got to leave. The menu's not attractive and the waitress is disconnected. Her feet are not on this floor. Anyway, she won't give a crap if I stay or leave. I've become invisible. To her, I, me, I do not exist other than as a source for a tip.

I chose depth, constancy, a life devoted to loving completely one soul. I shined in her radiance.

I am a moon in eclipse. I will leave. I am leaving. Maybe the back way is best. Street's too noisy, too busy. Too aggressive. It's different, this city is definitely not my city. Not the city we used to come to share.

What an alley. Rats, junk everywhere. The front so smart but this, disgusting. All a façade over this boiling bit of filth. Like the supermarkets, the hospitals, the political establishment. Will rats attack a human, will they run up my trouser leg? What's this pool, this rust coloured water? Maybe diluted blood. What bullshit that organic vegetarian joint…a cover-up for a slaughter yard. Even in these times probably not allowed.

Boys ahead. Look at the way they stand. Hunched like Neanderthals. Necks forward, sulphurous eyes glaring at me from below their heavy brows. Like a pack of prehistoric hunters. In the old days, I could take them on. I could beat them with my anger and strength. Anger and strength like a club with a spike. Not now. I think of her. Do I fear? Should I turn back? Can I retreat from fate? Is this fate? Maybe so, maybe not but joining her sooner than later is better now that I don't recognise the city, myself, life.

What is this? Fate? What fate? This is simply material reality. By chance a group of autistic traumatized kids with nothing better to do and nowhere safer to go, happen to be in front of me, blocking my way. All my understanding and concern…what do they care? My concern. Fighting the unfair system, fighting racism, fighting sexism, nationalism, confronting the brutes and bullies. But will that cut the ice with them? Will I be a man to look up to, cool, sacrosanct, a guru, a devil-may-care, a natural leader? They're mustering. My hair is grey now. The testosterone is running down their legs, filling their muscles with uncontrollable energy, leaving them helpless in the face of animal chemistry. My six-pack is buried under layers of life. They are shoving themselves away from the broken walls, the rusting railings, the rotting wooden bench. Shake a leg, boys, let's smear the opposition, the ponce, the other. Let's avenge. Let's entertain ourselves with the thrill of evil and the smell of blood. Hoods up, urban myths engaged, fear stalks the meek.

I can run. Run like a dart, run like a stream, like in my dreams but now maybe not. It's a confrontation of mind over matter, dreams over reality, ego over force, intelligence over aggression. The bright ones survive, the clever ones reproduced, and I am a consequence.

Do I remember Darwin? Survival of the Fittest. He meant the brightest, not the toughest. Let me tell these guys. But they seem stunted. Their lips dribble saliva as they spit foul words. I don't understand what they're saying. He swings. I hardly see it. Swift, abrupt, harsh and meant to stun. Blood rushes to my face. Has he cracked my cheekbone? Cut it. Sure, he's broken the skin. A serious business. Remember Darwin. And the whack to the back of the head. Unfair. Cowardly. I'm one, they're three. I'm old, they're young. I'm crippled with grief, they're careless with mirth.

I have this scrawny one by the throat. I could crush his windpipe, but my knees are giving way. The kick to the groin. I go down. Didn't want to hurt them. It's like not wanting to kill a chicken or a fish. Suppose I would if it came to it. All those carcasses in the windows, all those sweet lambs bounding in spring. No, better I should live to my principles rather than kill another sentient being.

These ants are unaffected by what we higher animals do. Marching, columns ragged but definitely ordered, coordinated, directed. Can I move? Well yes. But I hurt. Hurt. More pain as if I don't have enough but hey, who doesn't? Now to stand. This dirt, the clag of cities, detritus, the odours, smells, stinks, really a stench. The odours disgust me more than the rest of it. The acid colours, the screeching noise, the endless locomotion. But I can stand and pull my nose, my so sensitive nose away from its intimate relationship to the merde of life. My heart hurts. Not the hurt of a cardiovascular incident, not a casualty of stress, steroids, Western voodoo medicine or inherited dysfunction. It's the pain of carrying my version of humanity in my body.

Oh, it hurts to walk. My leg is dragging. I must look like a real bum. Dirty, stinking, clothes ripped.

My wallet. My identification gone. This alley is dark. Only the broken glass has life. There it reflects the seagulls. They are crying. But our city wasn't near the sea. Guess the gulls follow the river up. No identification. She's gone…go on say it. The word that leaves one empty and bereft…she is 'dead', and I am without her, I am alone without her lustrous beauty. I have no identification.

My heart like my clothes. More faithful. Sewing, stitches. Can't sew a heart. This isn't believable. What happened to yesterday? It was always going to last. There is just a heartbeat, a torn heartbeat between having her in my arms, smelling her sweet skin, the cardamom of her armpits and this empty alley. I want this to be a nightmare. I've always suffered from nightmares. Hands too big. Couldn't hold anything. Numbers, large numbers rushing at me from the dark. Bounding with great joy, running, sailing into the air, flying to my great delight, then realising, 'I'm out of control, I'm aiming for a dangerous landing'. My heart like torn cloth.

How can an alley be so long? How can there be so much broken glass? They shouldn't have taken my shoes. Cruel. Greasy overhanging walls. Greasy with age, with the ooze of sap, with pig fat having drained down the tiles. The fat of dead animals, the fat of obese people sweating out their guts. Dying the death of indulgences. Like a shambles. But where are they? I can hear them. The clang of pots, the distant TV with their sounds of seeming urgency, the sirens, the flies, the crying infants and boisterous children, the screaming women and shouting men, the squealing pigs, but where are they?

If she were here there would be an answer. She always knew and if she didn't, she made it up. But it was always somehow true. She couldn't lie. She found the truth even if by her imagination rather than deduction. And it calmed me. Seemed rational. Sure, it was good to talk. We always came to an agreement, a mutually accepted analysis. We acted on it. Hand in hand we acted in harmony. It was good, it made sense.

Men ahead. They've seen me.

Boys in the alley, old guy takes warning; men in the light, old guy takes fright.

She'd have known how to read this. One guy's stopped to lean on his shovel. Lighting a roll-up. The others, older, thickened, heavy canvas clothes. Workmen, salt of the earth. Workmen, digging, making something, constructing, rebuilding the ruins, making good a broken wall. They understand how to extend a helping hand. They've seen it all before…the suffering, the unemployment, the low wages, the death of the apprentice system, the cold winds of change, the frustrations, disappointed wives, angry kids; sure, they'll know how to extend a helping hand.

In my state, I gotta trust someone. Not sure about the young one, that shovel man, but the older guys can keep him in check. If I can't trust them it would prove my heart is empty. Torn clothes, ripped heart.

There's a park below. Not well kept but still a park. Dusty, needs some loving, trees need thinning, the Acers need cutting back, bald patches in the lawn but I should talk. A park right here adjoining this horrid alley. Rabbits, squirrels, maybe even deer. Silver birches, yellowing leaves dangling like pieces of gold or Christmas tinsel, tired Douglas Firs, a whole stand of them. Old men bent with the weight of their branches like old men bent with the tug of age. The earth calling, beguiling, torturing even. An entrance into the unknown but an entrance and so an exit from pain. That's speculation.

Help me down the ladder. Guess there're no stairs nearby. What a joke, of course I'll find my way out. Found my way in, didn't I? What's so funny? I wonder. Need permission from them to get in, permission, unlikely they say, to get out. What a set of jokers. Shovel man impassive. Guess I was wrong. He watches like a bruised hawk, haughty, impassive or maybe just tired.

Small lives, small trees, small hours. Darkness threatens like an ending of a life, like the dwindling of a dream, like a sentence falling away without meaning. Small lives, like mine has become. Like a ragtag, a down and out, a bum. There's a light. Civilisation, humanity, a kind of order in nature's dusty disharmony.

Leg hurts. I stink. How will I go on? Small lives care about such things. What happened to the concepts: freedom, equality, beauty, imagination? I used to speak about these things. They thrilled me but maybe because in her eyes I could appear noble, worthy, whereas I have always been just a spinning prism reflecting her warm light.

Funny, everyone's dressed the same. White gowns, no belts. White shoes even. I'm out of place. There is a design here, a grand plan. Order. Out of place with my small life. But yesterday I had no need to be accepted, to be legitimised by inclusion. She gave me strength. Without her, I am half a person and hardly a man. Defeated by a waitress, beaten by punks, intimidated by a kid with a shovel, frightened by shadows. Do I mind that he is laughing, and she is staring? Who are they to judge? So, I look poor and smell like a bum but who are they to judge?

I want out. A long corridor, green fluorescents, an institutional smell, a hospital smell. Brown lino creased by wheels. Yellow walls scraped by a thousand elbows. A flickering light. A distant door. Bars on the windows. Oh, bars on the doors.

I tell two men in white, two large men, I want out. They say, sure, everyone wants out. But they don't know me, I am here by mistake. They tell me everyone is here by a quirk of fate. I tell them there is no such thing, but they laugh and ask me why then am I here?

I think of her beauty. I think of her skin. I think of her perfumes. These are my jewels. Untradeable, inexplicable. I can feel the needle. I think of her skin. Someone has died. I think of her beauty. I remember her sigh. She whispered, 'we are one, there is no skin between us. We are one, just you and me.' She exhaled a warm breath and tickled my ear.

The needle goes deeper. We are one. I remember her sigh.

Therapy i: The Cat

B Thomas

A black cat jumped down from the wall where it has been sunning itself. January, and the sun low in the sky warmed the stone, then continued its journey directly through the therapist's window bleaching out any stray colour in the magnolia consulting room.

'Is that your cat?' I asked.

I didn't expect a reply, but it was fun to goad. It often provided good meat for the session. Now I'm wondering why I'm thinking about meat. If she asks me about my association with black cats I can say, *witches*, that will get us going. However, she didn't. She retained her professional silence and left me to flounder. Fishes now?

'Where are your thoughts?'

'I had a dream last night.'

I'll put her out of her misery I thought; I could feel from behind the couch her attention gathering. Whatever thought strings she was untangling in her cats-cradle of patients stories a dream always called her in. It was true, I did have a dream, and she was in it. In the dream I'd been walking with her, holding her hand like a small child, watching her watching, while two small fields of female bodies, buried just beneath the surface, were trampled by massive machinery. Oh no, I wouldn't give her the pleasure of that one.

'I was in the countryside, gently rolling hills and pleasant paths. I came across a man, youngish, thirties maybe, blonde, good looking. He was standing next to a tree; I understood he had planted it. It was very beautiful. I went on my way but later, with some others, I returned and stole the tree, pulled it from the ground and put it into the back of my estate car. Later, maybe the next day, the man came to me again; I felt waves of love for him. He said that he knew I had stolen the tree.'

The cat was back on the wall, I don't remember having seen it before. It stretched a back leg out and buried its face in its under-parts.

'You were telling me last week that you were dealing with solicitors about your late aunt's will.'

Clever, I thought.

'So, could this be a family tree?'

Well, I suppose it could. I should be talking about why I spend my time on her couch trying to hide anything deeper than a badly buried cat's turd, and paying good money for it, when I should be digging deep down and dirty.

There was coughing from behind me, it went on a bit. We had missed some sessions in December because of her bronchitis. I presumed the oxygen canister in the corner of the room was not there for décor, though I considered it a bit over-dramatic.

'You'll have to excuse me,' she spluttered 'I need a drink of water.'

'Yes, of course.'

Very seldom, if ever, had I been alone in this room. Was it a test? Was she looking at me now via a camera or a two-way mirror? There was a mirror on the wall to my right, unframed in oval shape with a moon and stars etched into one side. Underneath it, there were bookshelves with bound Psycho-therapeutic Association journals. Behind me were double doors that separated this area from her living space. I'd never seen her living space. The tiny house was part of a modern terrace built about ten years ago, squashed between a row of substantial mansions. The mansions where the terrace now stood had been allowed to crumble. Some scam. This house, where she lived and worked alone, I supposed, had three floors. On the ground floor was a tiny waiting room, and loo which I'd never used. Impossibly narrow stairs led to this room I was in. I presume she slept on the floor above. The standard fifty-minute sessions made it unusual for patients to meet. I'd never met one. Perhaps I was her only patient.

I could hear her hacking away in a downstairs room. I was sealed to the couch, with vague feelings of guilt (of course). Why didn't I sit up, browse her journals, even take a peep through the double doors? Bravely I did so, my mind teeming with childhood fears — *go to your bedroom, wait 'till you father gets home.*

Perhaps the coughing fit was a strategy to reveal my deeper neuroses.

She returned, apologised, sat down with her glass of water, and I lay down like a good girl.

'Are you feeling better?'

'Were you worried about me?'

Oh, for god's sake, why is it about her. I told her the old joke. 'Let's talk about you — what do you think of me?'

'So, you were angry that I left you.'

'No, I was worried about you.'

Was I? Not really. And on and on, la Ronde, churning drivel till she said, 'time's up.' I stood to go.

'See you on next week,' she said and handed me my monthly bill.

I returned at my appointed hour on Thursday determined to raise the subject of bringing my therapy to an end. After all, I was much better, or at least no worse for the two years I had spent on her couch. No sun this time. No cat. There was a cold drizzle and the wet pavements penetrated the soles of my boots. I rang the bell as usual and was surprised at how long I had to wait for the buzzer to open the front door. I questioned myself—was it Thursday? I rang again, and after a moment the door was opened by a man.

'Hello, do come in.'

I detected an American accent. I squeezed past him into the impossibly narrow hall. A patient leaving, I assumed and was curiously pleased that I was not the only one and that this chap looked totally normal, like someone who could successfully run his life.

'Do go on up.'

I did, and he followed, on the landing, where Joan would usually be waiting, having buzzed me in, her door was closed. I went to knock, and the man passed behind me and opened the door to her living room and invited me in.

At the kitchen end of the room, there were wooden units, the window above the sink which faced the street had a pretty blind and herbs on the window ledge. The back part of the room had a fireplace, a mix of easy chairs and a coffee table. Against the double doors which led to her consulting room was a large bookcase. Clearly, she never opened the doors, and they might be a sound-proofing element. There was no television. The room was sparse with Shaker-like comfort.

'Do sit down.' He indicated one of the chairs. He sat in the other one. 'My name is Clive—Joan's nephew. I'm afraid I don't know your name?'

I told him.

'I have some bad news.'

By now I was prepared. How clever of him to take his time. I'd have blurted it out on the doorstep.

'My aunt died last week. I'm sorry we haven't been able to find her patient contacts to let them know. But there again perhaps face to face is better. Had you been seeing Joan for a long time?'

'Two years.'

'I'm sorry it must be quite a shock.'

'Yes.'

'Would you like a cup of tea?'

'Thank you.'

He got up and went over to the little kitchen. The painting above the fireplace was a modern landscape, a patchwork of fields in umber and purple, with two small patches darkly ploughed. He returned with the tea.

'When did she die?'

'Last Thursday, in the night. A patient with an appointment on Friday morning raised the alarm.'

'I saw her last Thursday.'

'Yes, maybe you were the last person she saw.'

I drank my tea and wondered what I should do.

He continued. 'I arrived at the weekend, from Vancouver, I'm her only relative so I will stay and organise the funeral. If you let me have your details I will let you know when it is.'

'Thank you. Perhaps I should go now?'

'There's no rush. Is there anything you would like to take, a memento? I have to clear everything before returning home.'

'No thank you.' I stood up, I still had my coat on. I fastened it. 'Thank you for being so kind.'

He fetched a notebook from a small bureau in the corner. 'Would you write down your details for me?'

I wrote what he asked.

'Did Joan have a cat?'

'Yes.' He sounded surprised that I'd asked.

'Where is he?'

'She's upstairs. I'm going to take her to the people who re-home them.

'Right. Well, thank you again.'

'Would you like her?'

'What?'

'The cat? Joan's cat?'

'Oh yes. I think I would.'

'That's great, I'll get her.'

He went upstairs, and I was left wondering why I had said yes. My flat was minute, on the fifth floor with no outside space. The cat box hardly fitted down the stairs. I wondered about a coffin but knew I couldn't ask.

'Here she is, I'm so glad she's found a home.'

He went ahead down the stairs and left her on the pavement.

'I'll be in touch.'

The cat was complaining, it was raining quite heavily. He could have paid for a bloody taxi. I set off towards the tube.

Wolves ii: Perpetrator

M Kitton

The five-year-old Felan stumbled by the pond. His mother chased him, growling. The child squealed as she got closer to his unbalanced form.

'Mamma! Come catch me!' he shouted over his shoulder, silver eyes glowing with delight as he kept running around the pond before tripping on jutted out tree roots; sending him sprawling on the grass. He cried out in surprise, the grin falling from his face and looked up from where he had face-planted the floor. The shade of the trees sent a cool tickle down the back of his neck…

Short brown hair, glowing amber eyes, lean and fast. Otherwise known as one of the friendlier Wolves, who had volunteered to take Felan under his wing: this was Fridolf, the Gamma.

And Felan was sent on a job with him.

Well, it was less a job than robbing a shop on the corner of the street for money and alcohol for the Alpha.

They gathered all the necessary equipment before sprinting from the warehouse door and heading into the city centre. Their shadows morphed as they moved as a blur, the silhouettes never forming a solid shape, each one melting and joining with the other.

They stopped just down from the shop and stared above them at the faint pastel colours that painted the skyline.

'You ready Felan?' Fridolf smiled.

Felan grinned back. The adrenaline already thrummed through his veins, then faltered when Fridolf pulled a pistol from his jacket. The Zeta's eyes widened when he saw the pistol…Was Fridolf really going to use that?

Felan fumbled through his many layers of clothing and drew his dagger, the metallic blue metal shimmering in the light, sucking in the harmless colours of pink and orange. They could already hear sirens wailing far, far in the distance, maybe in pursuit of some other offender.

Felan gripped his knife tighter when he heard Fridolf loading his pistol before him.

They barrelled through the automatic doors. The Gamma pointed his gun at the shopkeeper. The Zeta hurried over to the alcohol cabinet and started filling his backpack frantically, including as much of the strong stuff as he could; he knew it put the Alpha out of it much quicker. Fridolf rifled through the till, breaking open another glass cabinet for random valuables. Felan's left hand shook so hard he almost dropped his bag containing over fifteen bottles — looking back now he was glad he didn't as the Alpha may have just murdered him. The Zeta clenched his eyes shut at the noise of the pistol being fired.

'Felan! C'mon let's go!' Fridolf yelled over the scream of the sirens. 'Felan. We need to go!'

Felan nodded shakily twice and followed Fridolf out of the shop, feet slapping heavily on the cracked concrete. He flinched when he heard the screech of brakes behind him, the bangs of car doors being kicked open. He glanced back as he went, and his eyes widened as he saw a dozen guns aimed right at them.

This wasn't supposed to happen… Right?

Bullets streaked passed them at different velocities, shattering windows as they whistled through the gaps between their heads and their feet.

Felan ducked to the left when he felt a sudden breeze beside his ear. He yelped, raised his hands to his head. He glanced at the Gamma, eyed the fork at the end of the street and howled. They tore down their different paths and his feet pounded down the narrowing alleyway.

He stumbled to a halt some twenty minutes later, muscles aching. He slumped against the wall and let his eyes slide shut as he caught his breath.

A figure leapt towards him out of the shadows, grabbed him around the neck and forced him over a shoulder. He landed with a heavy thump, momentarily winded. The bag slipped through his fingers, but he didn't hear any of the bottles smash. He tried to scramble to his feet, but the unknown force squeezed around his neck. He thrashed his body on the floor, flayed his legs out to try to get a good kick on his attacker, but he couldn't do anything. He brought his hands up to join those around his throat, fingers scratching and fighting to get access to air, looked up, saw the crazed blue eyes. A tramp—his ragged hair was sloppily cut at his shoulders, billowed in the wind, framed his face. His eyes swirled like a hurricane about to power through everything by force; they were fixed intently on him, staring all the way into the back of his skull.

A rusty knife appeared and started its descent on

Felan's throat, inching closer and closer. The man released the Zeta's neck, shoved an arm there instead, forced him flat on the ground. Felan pushed an arm weakly upwards towards the knife, tried to push it in the opposite direction, felt his hand slip and the knife descend further. He grunted, gripped it with both hands, content with pushing it away from him; not caring where it ended up anymore. His heart pounded. He kicked and fought…The man was far too strong, and it was clear that he was waiting for Felan to put up a better fight. The gap between the tip of the knife and his exposed neck shortened centimetre by centimetre. He made a last feeble attempt to push the bigger man off him. He didn't want that rusty knife anywhere near him.

He looked up, saw a manic grin, two rows of decayed teeth. It was all just a game. The tip of the knife pressed into his throat. He howled with the exertion, closed his eyes, pushed upwards suddenly. The man slipped sideways; for the moment, off-balance.

This was all the opportunity Felan required: his training came right back to him. He managed to arc his back enough that he could raise himself with one arm, losing the grip on the knife and jabbing quickly into the man's ribs. The man's head jolted upwards. Felan persisted, dug his elbow into his attacker's abdomen, the unexpected ferocity knocking him back. It gave Felan enough space to twist his arm into his back pocket to extract the knife he hid there. Unsheathing it, he pushed the man off him completely. He stumbled to his feet, gasped heavily as he placed a hand on the wall to keep himself standing. He eyed the man. He hesitated.

'Go to your room now!' His menacing voice reverberated throughout the empty house.

Felan frowned in confusion. 'But daddy…I wanna watch 'toons! Mamma said I could.' He was interrupted by a sharp stinging sensation on his cheek. He backed up and stared into his father's angry eyes, yelped as his wrist was grasped too tightly.

'Don't speak about her again Felan!' he shouted, laughing quietly as his son struggled. Another slap and Felan wrenched himself from his father's grip and bound up the stairs.

Felan closed the little distance between them and slashed the knife. A huge gash opened the man's chest, blood stained his filthy clothes, he snarled, backed away, astonished, eyes fearful.

The smug look was wiped clean off his face.

Felan sprang forwards, howled, and drove the

knife towards the man's unprotected chest, heard bones snap as it sank deeper and deeper, saw blood pouring from the wound as he pulled it back. The man grunted and sank to his knees.

Felan looked to his feet, saw the blood flow thicker, and watched fascinated as it twisted its way towards him like a snake. His ears rung. His heart throbbed. His body ached. He was mesmerised by the blood that sloshed about his feet.

Until it began to seep rather alarmingly up his trouser leg.

He spotted his bag, stashed poorly in a crack…he stumbled over to reclaim it. He checked the contents before he set off again.

No bottles had broken.

The Space

E J Jennings

That space was not there before.

It is a perfectly sculpted space formed through the geometry of carefully positioned leg guards and foot covers, purchased to protect my teenage frame from the pounding impact of hard little hockey balls. It is the space where my goalie helmet, over-shirt and left glove should be, have been, always go. It is the space where they were one hour before.

My mind, trained, sensitised, experienced with this madness, starts racing. One hour ago, hockey pitch, training, ending, list, always the list, my list of goalie kit, three times, pack it in, tick the list, take it out, tick the list, pack it in, tick the list, take it out, tick

117

the list, three times. Jean, coach, curious, why? Me, shrug, because, can't hurt. Interrupted. So, start again. Pack it in, tick the list, take it out, tick the list, and on. On. On.

Finish list. Three times. Calm. Zip bag, leave pitch, darkness, cold air, floodlights, Jean, me, walking, talking, just us, last people. Lock pitch, clang, cold metal gate, solid, padlock, no entry, no exit. Empty pitch, beautiful sheen, green, light, clear, pure, uncluttered. No things. No things on the pitch. None. All gone. In bags. On lists.

See Gary, see van. Hi Gary. Give Gary bag, enter sports hall. Leave bag in van, with Gary. Mum's boyfriend. Leave bag with him. Leave with him, not with me. Mum trusts Gary. He is nice to me. He buys me chocolate and CDs and sweets. Trust, breathe, leave bag in van with him. Go in hall for team meeting, handouts, information, ten minutes of information. Leave hall, get in van, go home.

Get home, cross threshold, feel fear. There were ten minutes with team. Ten minutes without bag. Must look, must know. Clutch list, open bag. Open bag in hallway with coat and shoes still on. Open bag before dinner, before shower, before 'Hello Mum'.

No…No! No! No! How? How!

There is a space. But there shouldn't be a space. But there is a space. Waves of silent panic start breaking across my diaphragm.

I must be mad...Truly, I must be. All these things missing. All these times. Why? Why can't I keep my things? Whhhyyyyyyyyyyyy? Whhhhhyyyyyyyyyyyyy?

My search for rationality is eclipsed by roaring inner wails of grief, keening wracking high-pitched wails sent up to the forces beyond my control that keep doing this to me. Where are they, these forces? Who are they? If there are bad ones, then can't there also be good ones? Where are the good ones?

Why is this happening! Why can't I look after my things! Please! Plleeeeaaaasseee help me!

Despair, alone in the hallway with the shoe rack and umbrellas, separated from my home by a thin white inner door with an ornate glass panel in its centre. I can see their shadows in the kitchen, Mum and Gary, moving across the shiny mottles like dark wavy shapes moving in and out of the coloured patches, from orange, to clear, to green, to clear.

I have to tell them, again. And I'll be punished. Again! I can't do this! I can't keep being punished like this, for things I can't control!

But in fact, it's not the punishment I fear most. I can cope with being grounded, I can cope with the shouting, and I can even cope with the judgement and shame. But it's the madness that I fear the most.

I collapse to my haunches and draw jagged shuddering sharp little breaths. Saliva drips from my panting mouth and I watch it unfurl and then dissolve in the doormat. The actions of a mad girl, surely.

I can't be mad. I can't. But who is taking my things then? I don't believe in ghosts, I don't believe in fairies... At least, I don't think I do. Do I? No, Ellie, no you don't. You don't believe in those things. They don't exist, they're not taking your things.

But then...What? I can't have lost it this time, can I? So many things! Can I?

The whirring starts to settle as my breathing finds purchase in reality. Time and space come back together, the present regains some lucidity, and my inhales extend as my exhales relax. I lift my head and stare, almost violently, at the clumps of mud on the bristles of the mat.

No.

No, I don't think I lost them, not this time. How could I have done? All the lists, all the checking. So much checking! But if ghosts and fairies don't exist, and if I'm not mad, then...

There is only one other explanation to be found. But it is so vile and so wretched. So very fucking wretched. Believing in fairies would be preferable! But if this is the truth, well…

One more check. Just one.

I move swiftly to the warm kitchen, alive with fajita spice and peppers frying, a table laid for three, the expectant cutlery arrangement of people hoping to find closeness through shared food and chatter.

'Hello, darling!'

'Hi, Mum.'

'What's wrong?'

'Nothing. I'm phoning Jean.'

'Oh, ELLIE! You haven't lost something again, have you? Not again for CHRIST'S SAKE!'

I stare directly at her.

'No. I haven't.'

The phone is ringing. *'Hi, Jean? It's Ellie. I know this will sound mad, but could you check if I left anything on the pitch?'*

'OH, ELLIE REALLY! You must be JOKING!'

Wide-eyed flaming incredulity from Mum, pausing mid-push of crackling peppers. Snorts and derision from Gary, rolling eyes, leering mouth, folded arms, and ironically shaking head, shame, shame, endless pits of painful gut-wringing shame.

'Yes Jean, I know I did my list…So, you won't look? … Yeah, no point…No, I'm ok Jean, thank you…Honestly, yeah. I'll call you tomorrow. Thank you. Bye.'

I click the phone into place and turn to face the blame that has come to be so familiar. They stand together as a unit, a wall of authority in front of the stove as the peppers fizzle out. The fear pulses strongly now, like always, pounding around my temples, ringing in my throat, shuddering in my chest and clouding my eyes as the combined force of confusion, shame and terror permeates my brain.

But this time there's a different tone amidst the cacophony, a strengthening of the voice that has always been speaking but rarely been heard. *You are not insane, Ellie.* This time I have found the truth, my truth, from the many thousand versions that have circled my head in these years. This time I will not be shamed.

'Gary. You've taken my things.'

They explode. Shrieking, shouting, arms, elbows and fingers flying and pointing and slashing the air with shock and outrage and anger, like jerking marionettes, unpredictable, disturbing and violent.

My body is numb now, frozen against the onslaught of aggression. I know there is no safety for me here.

Gary storms out of the kitchen with bluster and anger and outright denial. I don't know where he's gone, and I don't care. Limp with despair, Mum sinks to a chair, pushing cutlery aside, her head in her hands, completely and utterly spent. I can't smell the fajitas anymore.

'Mum…I'm so sorry. I can't… I have to…'

'Why are you doing this, Ellie? Why? After all that we have done for you! All of it! Everything! How can you be so selfish!'

'I have to go, Mum. I can't be here anymore. I have to go.'

The pain in my upper chest crescendos as I witness my mother, my deepest connection, my everything, slumping forward on the table unable to look at me. Staring blankly at the cloth, her wavy brown hair protrudes from the gaps between her fingers as they cradle the weight of her head. Silence fills the space and the resonance in my chest is bordering on unbearable. But she is slumped towards the kitchen window, a tall white-framed rectangle reaching right up to the high ceiling of our narrow, Victorian terraced house. The night is so black and huge out there, so shiny and cool and spacious. I know that it's there I must go. The resonance in my chest abates as I realise I have endured enough, and that I deserve to be free.

I'm sorry, Mum.'

My whisper hangs softly as I turn from the kitchen, leaving her crumpled and bathed in yellow light from a round glass-shaded bulb. I tiptoe out, sensitive to her pain but unable to hide the growing momentum born of my imminent liberation.

Leaving the kitchen (*I did it!*), walking the hallway (*I fucking did it!*), climbing the stairs *(ba-STARD, ba-STARD, ba-STARD)*, entering my room (*I'm out of here! Now! Tonight! I'm free!*).

Go, Ellie. Go. Now. Bag, pants, socks, diary, Winnie, toothbrush, toothpaste, (*Dad's is so gross*), phone, charger, t-shirt. *That's it, Ellie. Go. Now.*

Down the stairs, placing my feet gently. Now is no time for stomping. Pausing at the bottom, Mum is still in the kitchen. Still bent. Still slumped.

'I love you, Mum. But I'm going now.'

Silence.

I turn, see the door, walk towards it, open it. I am gone.

The night air surrounds me like a plunge into ice. It is so fresh, so clean, so beautiful, so utterly exhilarating to be out of that house.

I am the master of my destiny! I am queen of my world!

I run, sprint, bound, leap along the ancient Saxon grass banks that enclose our town, the amber street lights casting just enough glow for guidance. Dark trees rush past, dog walkers startle, gravel crunch-crunches, and my feet just pound, pound, pound, pound, lithe, fast, powerful. I am engorged with agency, I am enthralled by my choice, I am a pulsing body of wild flowing energy moving to a place where I know I am welcome, where I know I am safe.

Rounding the corner to the cottage I am breathless, flushed and thrilled. I slip down the old stone side passage, and veer right along the back of the little terraced row where I thrived for thirteen years. Home. Ducking into our yard I see him at the sink, the moving part of a radiant window-framed scene of warm wood and cosy kitchen, shining out against a night of shadowed bricks, moon tinted slates and darkened coal sheds. He's washing his plates and boiling his water for his cup of tea in his Smarties mug that he'll drink in his lounge with the books and the fire and the records and rugs.

I knock on the door and he startles but moves to meet me straight away. I can hear him unlatching the inner wooden door and sigh in relief at the gentle sshhhhhhh of the brush hairs along its bottom, sweeping the kitchen lino as it opens.

Ker-chunk-chunk.

The front door Chubb and latch release together, a jolted swish of opening, and there he is. Dad. Gruff, strong, solid, present, and looking a bit confused.

'Are you alright?'

'Not really, Dad.'

'Do you want to come in?'

'Yeah, please.'

I flop into my chair at the end of the wooden table, by the wooden stairs that Dad made, opposite the aged stove that he salvaged from the tip and that, by all accounts, should have been condemned long before. He pours me a cup of tea and we go through to the little lounge, with the books and the fire and the record and rugs. It's different since Mum and I left. We just left him one chair on the day we moved out, a big black leather chair that was worn on every edge and creaked metallically when he sat in it. I watched him pull it into the middle of the room that day, creating eight feet of air between each point of the chair and the telly and the bookcase and the fireplace and the walls, resting on the mustard carpet with a wooden table to one side.

But he's repopulated the room now. There's a hand-me-down floral sofa from his sister and a new wooden fireguard that he's knocked up in his shed, plus a wicker chair and reed-patterned cushion in the corner by the spirits cabinet with the many different whiskies.

'So…you think he's taking your stuff then, do you?'

Everything tumbles out, all the stories of things gone missing, my confusion and doubts and fears. Dad listens, mostly, and nods very occasionally. He knows Gary. He sees him around town and he knows his games: covertly smoking in side alleys

126

and then frantically chewing gum so that Mum won't notice the smell later on.

'Sounds like he's been taking you for a ride, doesn't it…?'

'Yes Dad, I think he has.'

'Hmmmm…well, it's late now. Let's sleep on it and see what tomorrow brings.'

'Yeah, ok. Is my bed made up?'

Although it isn't really my bed anymore. Dad has moved it to a different wall and turned it round ninety degrees. My little desk is gone too, along with the sun-moon wind chimes and Pink Panther poster. And my lovely long shelf of cuddly toys is bare too, its emptiness demanded in tandem with mine and Mum's exit. Just a Beano sticker remains, in the bottom left pane of the old sash window, half scratched off but otherwise immovable, undeniable. There are no mobile things in this room, there is nothing I have to protect. Closing my eyes in the dark, I know that this is bliss.

I wake with the light and adjust to the newness of old sounds forgotten. The latches of the inner doors, the sweeping of Dad's slippers on the lino, the rattling of metal against metal in the kitchen sink. I head down for breakfast, relishing the creaks of the old wooden stairs. The second from bottom is my favourite because it changes in tone from left (short high creak) to right (long low groan). Sometimes I roll one foot from side to side just to hear it change.

Dad is getting the cereals out and putting them on the counter. There aren't any Lucky Charms of Frosties any longer, but Shredded Wheat and Weetabix are a treat that morning. With fresh milk and soft banana and tea from the little brown pot that's filled thousands of our cups. I hop back in my seat at the end of the table and start swinging my legs. They're far too long, of course, but I lift them up just to feel their weight and their arc as they bump against the chair legs. Dad gives me a look but carries on at the sink.

Suddenly there's a shadow at the window. Gary has appeared in our tiny backyard, with the coal shed and fish pond and lovely old stone paving. He's smiling in through the window, all sunbeams and laughs, waving colourful bits of plastic in the air of varying shapes and sizes.

Rooted, numb and immobile on my chair I watch Dad flick his hands in the sink, dry them on a tea towel and move to the door. He is out of sight now and I can just see Gary through the window. There are muffled rumbles of older men in discussion. I can't hear their words, I don't want to hear their words. I can't swallow my Weetabix anymore.

They finish. Gary is all jovial and smiles, waving at me through the window, grinning to show the gaps between his few stumpy teeth. He turns and swaggers from the yard, closing the gate carefully behind him with a last glance in my direction. A growing nausea pulses through my otherwise rigid body.

Dad returns to the kitchen, his arms laden with brightly coloured things. Three things. A brand-new goalie helmet. A brand-new over-shirt. A brand-new left glove. He places them on the counter by the cereals — and turns to me.

'What's all this about then?'

'I don't know, Dad…'

'I mean, why would he do this?'

'I don't know, Dad…'

'I mean, it doesn't make sense, does it! Why would he take your things and then buy them again?'

'I don't know, Dad…'

'Are you sure Ellie? I mean, are you really sure about this? It doesn't seem right to me…I think you've got this one wrong.'

The bottom drops out of my world. There is nowhere left to run.

The Cabin

H Evans

Log entry: 21.3.2017
The sun is always shining above the clouds—I'd always liked that line. No idea where it came from, only that it was spray-painted haphazardly on a burnt-out oil drum outside the once local Sainsbury's. I was crouched behind a couple of dead oak trees on the heath overlooking the parking lot, perhaps 250 metres from the entrance. Many of the surrounding buildings were derelict, ransacked or demolished. I thumbed the bolt of my .22 subconsciously while scanning the scene through an old optical scope atop the rifle. 17 more minutes. 17 more minutes until I'd creep on to the roof and let myself in to the abandoned employee mess area above the main

shopping floor. The sun sat lazily at 3 o'clock in the sky.

I'd repeat this ritual whenever I needed dried food, booze or smokes. Usually once a week. Since everyone vanished I'd taken up smoking as a kind of crutch, the taste was awful, but I had, in the 14 months since this shit went down, started smoking a couple of Marlboro Golds before bed. Took the edge off I guess.

Movement in the left peripheral corner of my vision. I swept the rifle sideways and scoped out a fox jolting across the roof of one of said abandoned houses. How the fuck did it get up there? The roof had to be 4 metres off the ground. Something felt a bit off. I scanned the area around the house, judging it to be about half a kilometre from my hiding spot. The fox bounced out of sight, and I couldn't find the source of my sudden uneasiness, so I let my breathing slow a little. Probably just chasing one of those flightless birds. 9 minutes.

I'd kept my generator running for the entire 14 months by syphoning from the local petrol station. During the first couple of months, when Google's servers were still online, I'd frantically searched and copied all the survival know-how I could stomach and stored both soft and hard copies. One of the first priorities in this information harvest was how to keep my electricity running. I'd known that I'd likely need hydrocarbon, so calculated how much was available. The local station had 4 pumps, two petrol and two diesel. This likely meant two subterranean tanks, 2 pumps a pop. Google had told me that each tank stored between 21,000-22,000 litres, so if I was lucky and the tanks were full, I'd have about 40,000 litres of fuel. After scrambling around in the depths of the station I totalled up 33,565 litres remaining. Not bad. I'd found a portable 10kW diesel generator in the local hardware store, pillaged it and driven it back to my cabin in my pickup. I didn't think Sam & Sons would be overly bothered, wherever they were(n't), but sorry boys. The generator burnt about a litre per hour at ¼ load, giving me 2.5kWs to play with—more than enough. I had about 4 years of easily accessible fuel, in theory. In the 13 months since, I'd been careful and only spent 6 months' worth by turning the generator off at night, so I was good—for now. 0 minutes.

I stopped daydreaming and lazily got up, slinging the rifle along my spine, before vaulting the fence in front of me. The trees I'd been hiding behind had once been in someone's garden, but nature had reclaimed much of the town at this point—rows of houses now opened into one expansive tangle of trees and brambles, and random god damn hidden fences. I was wearing a brown leather trench coat, black beanie and fingerless gloves. I looked full blown Fallout 3, but it wasn't for show — this coat was good camouflage and freaking warm. It had been a while since I'd come across any *others*, but it paid to be prepared. I reached the dead supermarket and climbed the drain pipe rungs until getting to the roof. The maintenance door was just as I'd left it last week, slightly ajar with an empty Kronenbourg lodged in at floor level. I kicked the can off the roof in a perfect arc (us wasteland wanderers have to keep occupied somehow) and walked down the staircase to the staff rooms.

I grabbed a warm can of Kronenbourg from the table, cracked it open and sipped it on the way to the staff kitchen. My heart leapt into my throat. A small child was hunched over, facing away from me, gorging herself on the remaining supply of Nik Naks. She hadn't noticed me, and I began to slowly back out of the room, fumbling at the butt of my rifle. I dropped the beer can in my haste, and the girl's head snapped around inquisitively. I didn't like the look in her eyes, if you could call them eyes. Her upper teeth were yellowed but intact, her skin a twisting palette of greys and reds. The next 3 seconds played out in slow motion as my body dosed itself with adrenaline. She leapt the room's 5-metre breadth in the first, I rifle butted her in the second, and ran in the third. The rifle butt had given me a bit of a head start, and time fast-forwarded to me sprinting away from the building as the girl jumped the roof, landing perfectly, apparently unharmed. In retrospect I was fucked at this point, the girl was less than 30 metres away. I had time for a single shot. I stopped running and chambered a round in my rifle, swiftly aimed and pulled the trigger. The girl's head exploded mid-sprint, skull fragments and blood showering the overgrown pavement. The momentum of the round picked the child's small frame up and threw it against the building's outer wall.

I wasted no time and didn't look back as I sprinted the entire 2 kilometres back to my cabin in the woods. Last time I killed, I had to lay low for days as they hunted me. I'd spent a lot of time making my cabin unrecognisable from the surrounding untamed mess of brambles, so I figured I was safe. They had limited cognitive abilities from what I could discern in my limited sample size of terrifyingly short encounters, and I'd never been followed back to the cabin before. What they did have was a pack mentality. If you saw one, it could be safely assumed there were more in the immediate vicinity. I'd never been caught by one, through sheer luck—but I figured it would be BAD if one of those things had me in its grasp. I mean a young girl—she must have been 8 years old—just jumped 5 lateral metres in a single second.

Nothing good could come of that.

Upon reaching the cabin, I carefully stepped over the bell-warning tripwires I'd hooked up and quietly swung the camouflaged wooden door shut. It wasn't even 4 o clock, but I didn't dare turn on any lights, instead, I sat on the planed wooden floor until my eyes adjusted to the low lumen levels.

I pulled out my android smartphone, which I charged religiously if only to play stupid games to pass the time (the phone networks were the first of the infrastructure to go down), and stared longingly at the empty signal bar, as always. I'm not sure how long I sat there playing Tetris on my phone, but after a few runs, I was on a roll. Beating your high score on Tetris, when you've been playing it solidly for 14 months, is nigh-on impossible, but I was in the game. I could feel the rows aligning as I smashed my previous record, silent fist bumping myself in the darkness of the cabin. Yes, the Google play store went down before I could download any other games, meaning yes, I was stuck playing this shit forever.

It was at this point that some rude fucker ran headlong into the outer wall of the cabin, with a distinctive crunch. I sighed, pocketed the trusty Tetris handset and gazed out of the left wall's hidey-hole. Nothing.

After an hour or so, I figured it was safe to resume my solitary status-quo, but instead of booting up the generator I lit my gas camping stove and emptied some tinned Sausages 'n' Ketchup Smash into a pan. I lit a cigarette off the stove and lay on my back as the 'meal' simmered and warmed. I wolfed down the reconstituted meat with a crushed-up vitamin tablet and spent the rest of the evening staring down the scope of my rifle, through the various hidey-holes I'd carefully carved out of each of the four walls of the cabin.

Log entry: 22.3.2017 - 2:13am
I woke up suddenly in pitch darkness, my forehead rubbed raw from resting idiotically on the barrel of the rifle. Hitting my phone told me it was 2:13 AM. I am a heavy sleeper, so something substantial must have woken me, though in the blurry, semi-hungover state in which I awoke—my brain was lagging. A loud bell ring sounded through the woods outside, one of my traps then. At this point, the fear was overridden by the annoyance of being woken up

136

at such an hour. Why can't anyone let the only remaining human get a decent night's sleep in his cabin? I groaned loudly, unsheathed my 6-inch hunting knife and threw the front door open in a rage.

Fifteen metres from the cabin was a pack of 4 wolves. Their eyes were pulsating, bloodshot white orbs which seemed to emit a small amount of light.

'WHY DOES EVERYTHING HAVE TO HAVE MESSED UP EYES?!' I screamed.

The wolves made no attempt to attack me and seemed genuinely confused by my exclamation. They just stood there, licking their chops, staring.

I walked up to the wolves and disembowelled the leftmost one with the knife, opening its chest from neck to breast. It died silently. The other wolves turned to watch with fascination. This was ridiculous.

'Nothing? You don't give a shit that I just went full Jason on your friend here?'

The three soulless pairs of eyes gazed expectedly at me. I plunged the knife into the ears of two more wolves, piercing the skull and killing them both instantly.

I woke up at 8 am and chuckled at the ridiculous dream I'd just had. I opened the door and gazed down. There were *white stains all over the floor.*

Log entry: 22.3.2017 - 9:45pm
The whole day was a struggle. Convinced I was losing it, I didn't dare leave the cabin, and sat huddled by the gas stove. Those wolves were real, as was my cold-blooded detachment.

Typically, I was a mellow, empathetic kind of guy, so sociopathic behaviour not only made no sense but truly scared me.

I used to lovingly foster my sister's unwanted kitten litters for god's sake.

Log entry: 25.4.2017
I finally emerged today and figured I could ease my paranormal fears by engaging in some back-breaking physical labour. I therefore spent all day chopping and hauling timber to the cabin to make some structural improvements.

The cabin itself is a single square room, measuring 4 metres along each wall. The foundations are large timbers industrially driven into the rough soil. Without a pile driver, extending the cabin was going to be a back-breakingly manual job. I'm a little out of shape so the labour should toughen me up a little — being fit was something I'd realised was important about a week after this shit went down, when I'd hauled all the necessary belongings from my 4th floor flat to the cabin.

Needless to say, I was a mess of hot sweats in under an hour of filling up the truck.

The idea is to build a bathroom, 2x2 metres along the south wall. To achieve this, I need eight solid foundation timbers, and a couple dozen smaller timbers to lay the walls and roof, round-log style.

Luckily, the county councils in Southern England decided, a while ago, to introduce Scots Pine to the local heathlands, both for their straight timbers and environmental impact. Turns out the cabin me and dad built was right in the middle of one of said heathlands, clever dad.

I think it'll take me a few days to chop the necessary timbers, and probably the better part of a week to manually drive the foundations.

Log entry: 07.05.2017 - 10:11pm
The foundations are finished after long days of digging and manually driving wooden piles with a sledgehammer. I could've finished it sooner, but I've been careful to take regular patrol breaks to check the trapped perimeter for unwanted guests. I also began digging a latrine for what will hopefully be a homely (if somewhat medieval) sitting-toilet.

Going to hit the sack early tonight, my back is killing me.

She

O Goodall

When she woke she woke from uneasy dreams to bright white light, the sun flooding through the fabric of the white curtains, *illuming* the room. A *revivification* after the night's slumbers. The morning sprawled through the window and she was in bed, wakeful, taking it in. The room was light and clear, and she lay a while. Enjoying the way the light reflected off the many colourful posters on the white walls.

She brushed the hair from her eyes, ripped back the white covers and rolled off the double bed, walked over to the window and pulled back the curtains to look at the beautiful sunshine and the day, the rich blue sky spreading over the city.

An enormous hand was descending from far above, rupturing the *quotidian* morning. With definite purpose, it moved steadily toward the window. Its shades and contours were conspicuous and stylised, as of a drawing or animation. Framed within the limits of the window, she could not move her feet. Gaining speed, the hand shot towards her.

She crashed to the floor beneath the window as the hand smashed through the glass. Shards and splinters, plaster and dust, fell atop her along with pieces of brick. The groping thing just above her sprawled and turned. Grabbing and grasping. Her room wreckage. She coughed and scrambled, bruised and half-crawling, and gasped along the edge of the wall away from the window towards a corner. She crouched there trying to make herself as small as possible, shrinking into the corner, cringing from the hand.

Violence. The hand juddered and flopped and jumped, snatching. The mirror was *cast* into the corridor where it exploded. The desk was shattered next to the window, the bed skewed and broken-looking against the far wall. Papers and posters swirled and flew chaotically in the dust frenzied by the hand's convulsions, the walls naked now.

The hand turned ranging to the corners, flailed ever wider. Trying to grab her. She inched toward

141

the window, keeping down. The hand pulled back suddenly and she leapt into the corner to avoid it. It pulled out to the now jagged opening, then plunged again into the room with renewed violence. Gasping and with tears in her eyes, she looked imploringly around. She had no idea what to do: how does one deal with the *absurd*?

She flattened herself to the floor under the window. And almost cut her hand on a pair of scissors. Debris from the shattered desk, they lay half-open. She gripped them shut, rolled over face up and brushed the hair from her eyes, then plunged the point hard into the soft palm of the hand coming down on top of her. It screamed a silent pain.

Terror. Frozen. Blood spattered her face as the hand thrashed manically.

She retreated, half-crawling, to slump into the corner once more. She still wielded the scissors defiantly, but hope was draining. She waved them wildly when the hand neared her. But the thrashings were losing force, strength draining like blood. The hand began to slump and then dragged itself defiantly out the broken window of her chamber.

And all the while I, sat in my corner (*my position* of *enunciation*), not helping. Scribbling in my notebook, weaving her into my story.

She stood up. She cast her eyes over the chaos of the chamber and moved over to the gaping window and looked out. At the beautiful sunshine and the day. At the stitched blue sky stretching over the city.

Arnica *(notes for a story)*

G Frosh

He was a big man, wide though, not tall. Mr Five by Five they'd called him at the abattoir.

Schlepping carcasses to the cold-store—his introduction to the joys of the flesh.

He worked hard, grafted, and in time, built a thriving business as a kosher butcher.

A relish for the product and the handling of it, his beaming good humour, and the oft-repeated mantra, …'Nothing but the Best…', had endeared him to his customers, who flocked from all over north London. A success, he was, a beacon to the community…and a special hero to his new wife, Rose.

Though sweetly pretty when young, in time her angel bow lips had lost their generosity, the sparkle and girlish joy which had once so entranced him, more elusive now, dulled, somehow become distant, aloof. He seemed not to notice and, still enfolded in some remembered vision of her, was insensible to the change, and to what might now be her disappointments.

They had excitedly planned for many children, but it hadn't come about, and though his adoration of her was undimmed, imperceptibly, the focus of it shifted to the form of their only child, Rebecca…Ever more so as she began to blossom from childhood…

He continued to prosper. The family proud, warm, close, secure in what appeared an almost impregnable comfort…until, that is, the calamity — the sudden loss of his beloved Rose

He was stunned, desolate, his ox-like shoulders ever more slumped as the realisation took hold, and he seemed to lose all sense of himself. Devoted customers started to notice that the spark had evaporated, his old commitment no longer there. Pretty soon the business was gone too.

He was reduced to picking up odd jobs in the meat trade, but it was no life compared to what had gone before. Very occasionally, there was a glimmer of joy, a fine piece of flesh in his hands, maybe a left-over from some large order. On rare occasions, he'd splash out himself and buy a small portion of something really special.

Rose would have loved it as much as he. It had been such a pleasure to recreate the food of their youth, of their mothers...dishes with origins almost lost, like vivid snapshots, but blurred with memories of some colourless 'Old Country'...hard to place or to decipher.

There was a particular joy if calves' livers were involved: calves' liver with onions, onions gently frying in chicken-fat...softly caramelising...the rich smells percolating up from the kitchen, the whole house seeming to acquire a sumptuous glow.

It was an expression of a love, a comfort, and with which they enfolded their beloved daughter, Rebecca...Rivka.

As a tiny thing, she had lingered, silently, in a corner of the kitchen, eyes wide, entranced by the clattering of pans and the sizzling, rapt and engrossed by the magic that was being made...But as she grew, and it became apparent that she was destined for great things, so it was also clear that her future would transcend the confines, even of that richly flavoured alchemy.

They were to become so proud of her and yet, at the same time, puzzled. Even before Rose had passed on, they already understood that their daughter's education, which seemed to them in part an expression of their own achievement, had created some sort of separation in the family. Not at all because Rivka had outgrown them, but somehow....it was as if she seemed never to be quite 'there' any more. Literally, this was so, because, on returning to London, instead of finding somewhere handy, close to home in Stamford Hill, she had, inexplicably, chosen to place herself almost as far away as possible. South of the river, as alien to them as it was distant, and where Their People were few and far between.

REBECCA

She is in her late forties but looks younger. With thick dark hair, like her mother's, though slightly unkempt.

More often than not, she's wrapped in a tweedy 'swagger coat', whatever the weather, frequently appearing to have forgotten she has it on. At times it's as if she's about to be engulfed/ drowned/ devoured/ overwhelmed by it…

She has an Oxbridge degree in anthropology and, for want of anything else, had started on a PhD at Sheffield (*something to do with kinship, myth, obscure tribal practices?*)

About four months in, nervous and feeling out of her depth, she got drunk at a faculty party...something confusing happened...and she thought she was pregnant.

That conviction lasted longer than it should have, and by the time she recognised that there would be no consequence, and partly in disappointment, she slumped rather—and never completed her dissertation...

There is a vagueness about her, unfocused...

Part of her confusion results from being distracted by nameless fantasies—perhaps daydreams—and on one such occasion, lost in some such narrative and lacking concentration, she stumbles down the steps leading to her basement flat. A great throbbing bruise appears on her thigh.

A neighbour, with whom scarcely a politeness has ever been exchanged, witnesses her distress and, half remembering a connection to the treatment of bruises, kindly digs out Arnica pills, a leftover from some long-ago involvement with a homoeopath.

At times Rebecca thought to be a vegetarian. *Whether this was a matter of principle, revulsion maybe, at the idea of slaughter...or perhaps, for her, it was connected to something closer to home?*

It was never clear in her mind...but when sad, or feeling fragile, she did find comfort in flesh—meat that is—which for her signified a desire to return to the warmth and safety of her family. But that particular instinct always remained unfulfilled, brought up short by something inexplicably akin to panic—warning her off…

She fingers the Arnica in her coat pocket, amongst the fluff….and by touch, unconsciously assumes it to be lip-salve—which reassures her…though she never thinks to apply it to her lips.

We gradually become aware that something unacceptable might have happened when Rebecca was younger, at least this appears to account for her confusion, her adriftness…but she can not/will not address or revisit it…or…perhaps it was simply something Rose had said, possibly just a sour throwaway, a casual aside, maybe, which Rivka had misinterpreted, the scattered words tumbling around in her head…long after Rose's passing…forever re-arranging themselves…

Maybe the cause of Rebecca's distress, sustaining the bruise and obscuring our view…

…our clear sight of it.

Therapy ii: A Party

B Thomas

I woke early IN JOAN'S HOUSE. IT WAS NICER THAN MINE. AND SHE WOULDN'T KNOW, now would she? It was raining. Lileth, after a brief trip to the garden, traipsed mud all over my duvet and settled down for the day. Clearly, she was going to be no help. I called Johnny and warned him about the extra guest.

'That interfering old bat you told me about?'

'Yes, she isn't old.'

'Ah, "new best friend"?'

'No! But she's broken her ankle.'

'So?'

'Well she did it here, she slipped on my rug.'

So I told Johnny all about hearing the crack, the ambulance, and that it wasn't life threatening but pretty dramatic all the same. He still didn't see why she had to come to dinner. He said was meeting the boys at the bar at seven, so they'd get to me about eight.

I'm not the best of cooks, I watch the television stuff, but I don't get much opportunity to try things out. Everything seems to get in such a mess when I cook, whereas they have neat bowls of this and that and the other. Anyway, I'm up to my elbows in suet (I'd decided on steak and kidney pie) when Marion called.

'Deirdre darling, I've run out of tea bags I forgot to put them on the list could you just …?' Next was, 'I can't get down to plug in my computer could you pop…?', then, 'Sweetheart (!) I've dropped my crutch down the stairs …' After which I turned my phone off.

I had to stretch the suet to cover the pie dish that I'd pre-cooked the steak and kidney in; it didn't look very pretty but I prayed it would taste ok. I scrapped the idea of canapés. It was going to be smoked salmon on brown bread and butter. Easy-peasy. Then I realised I hadn't done a veg. Fuck — corner shop and a packet of frozen peas; I said no home should be without them. I got back just in time to see

151

Lilith finishing the last of the smoked salmon. The air was blue, and I chucked a saucepan which missed, but sent her scudding back upstairs pretty damn quick. The corner shop wouldn't do smoked salmon. The kitchen sink was piled high with dishes and the floor covered in flour, and it was half past seven. There was a bottle open that I'd used in the pie, so I took a slug. The kitchen was a car crash, which wouldn't have mattered if it hadn't been open plan — the table wasn't put up, let alone dressed with Marion's linen and fancy plates, and I was in desperate need of a shower. I called Johnny, I think he caught the tremble in my voice, he told me to calm down, the food would be great, and as long as there was plenty of booze who'd care anyway, and I should stop being so middle class and go and have a shower, and he'd collect some smoked salmon on the way. What a friend.

Lilith glowered at me from the duvet as I came from the shower. I called her another rude name, but softer this time, I mean what cat wouldn't eat salmon, she must have thought I'd meant it for her as a treat. Now she'd be confused. Oh god, what would Joan say? Or she say to Joan? I was convinced she had a link to the spirit world. I decided to win her round by consulting her on my wardrobe for the evening. She quite liked the green silk skirt with little bolero jacket—I was a vintage shopper supremo. The black satin with sequins she dismissed out of hand; we were both unsure about the harem pants with embroidered top; eventually, we settled on 1950s red velvet shirt-waister with net petticoats.

The doorbell rang. So, no make-up. As I rustled down the stairs to the living room level I smelt the burning, I dashed in and rescued, mostly, the pie: it only had a little burn on the crust which was now the size of a milk bottle top floating on the gravy. But it did smell good. A rather more insistent ring on the door. Right, here goes, down and opened the door. Richard and Connor (Those are Johnny's mates. I quite like them) either side of and supporting Marion, and Johnny behind carrying a large box.

'Hello!'

'Get in quick! It's vile out here.' Johnny called from the back.

'Quick? Pas possible parce que lady brokky leggy' said Connor.

'Just far enough to shut the door.'

I went first up Joan's narrow stairs to the wreck of the week.

'Mmm, that smells good' said Johnny supportively as he put down his box.

He produced two bottles of champagne. 'Madam at *Tootsies'* (the bar where he worked) 'produced those, I told her it was my folks' silver wedding anniversary.' Then he produced a pair of speakers and a hub for our music. 'Music, song, who do you fancy? Don't need to answer that, Marion,' wagging his finger at her.

He found sockets and set it up. Lady Gaga filled the room, Richard was sprawled on the floor beside Marion, who was coiffured to perfection, and delighted, it seemed, with his stories. Connor was setting up the picnic table, linen cloth, napkins, wiping glasses till they shone and producing from somewhere a posy of violets. I was buttering bread for the salmon. Johnny popped the champagne corks and the party was in full swing. Connor and Richard thought the house was divine and they were going to start looking for something similar in the area straight away. Marion said she knew the local estate agents. I cooked the peas in the microwave and we all sat down on wobbly picnic chairs to a steaming plate of steak and kidney with a five pence size bit of slightly burnt suet pastry and perfect peas.

'Were these the peas you used on my ankle?' piped up Marion. The others looked a bit shocked.

'No, they went off in the ambulance.'

'Huff,' she said, or something like it. 'I call that theft.'

Everybody was enjoying themselves, especially me. I swished to the kitchen in my Doris Day dress, (though her kitchen would never have looked like this) and rustled up cheese and fruit. We sang along with Madonna, then Connor said we should have a competition. He had a new karaoke app on his phone. When he saw slight dismay around he said we should have two teams and Marion should be the judge. I was paired with Connor, with Johnny and Richard the other team. We cleared the room; the kitchen now was a cordoned danger zone and probably a health hazard as well. Marion was helped to her armchair. Both teams then had twenty minutes to choose their song and come up with a performance. Connor and I went upstairs to rehearse. He chose Shirley Bassey, (of course) *'Get This Party Started'*. The words were simple enough, so I was learning them, and he was looking for gear to wear. He tried a scarf round his head turban like, then I had a sudden thought. I beckoned him to follow me as I tiptoed to the holy of holies.

'Jesus, what's happened here?'

'That's how they left it. Clive said not to touch. Sssh.' We giggled, and I pulled back the sliding doors on the gowns I had discovered earlier. I thought he was going to faint with pleasure.

'What do you mean? Wear one of these.'

'Yeah.'

'Wow.' He pulled out a cream taffeta, encrusted with stones. I've never seen anyone get stripped so quickly, not for this purpose anyway. The zip wouldn't go all the way up, but we found a fur stole that covered the back. By this time, they were shouting from downstairs for us to get on with it. We quickly chose a green silk number for me and I fetched a couple of large candles from the bathroom. We crept downstairs and through the closed doors, I told them the number that we were singing and that we had to go first, and that when the track started they were to turn the lights off.

All went to plan and as the instrumental intro began Connor strode in with the candle illuminating his face like in the video of the track. He mimed to the first verse, *I'm coming up* …then when it moved to the chorus, I snapped the lights on and joined him. All three of them whooped with applause, then my bit. *Pull up to the bumper, get out of the car, License plate says stunner, number one superstar.* We didn't quite get through it all, it was so hysterical. Marion with some hairs now straying from her tightly controlled chignon was clapping and yelling *Get This Party Started* over and over. Through the din, somebody said, 'Shush, shut up, isn't that the doorbell?' The track had finished anyway. We were quiet. There was quite an insistent ringing on the door.

'It's the thought police.'

Brief hilarity.

'It's the noise squad!'

'Better answer it,' said Marion looking at me.

'I'm not going.'

'Well, I can't.'

Richard got up. 'I'll go, keep the noise down.'

We did keep it down, we were straining to hear what was going on. We heard him coming back up, the door opened and in it was framed a young person, muffled in layers of clothing with a balaclava, and a rucksack on her back that was larger than she was. We couldn't see Richard behind.

'Hello,' she said. 'I'm Terri.'

'Right,' I said. 'Who…?'

Dim Now, Getting Brighter

E Ruby

It was summer in England and all the leaves dripped with a wintery grey light. Time moves slowly in high densities, so the passing of it was a laborious, stolid event. There were too many options: the laptop, the games, the phone and the freedom of a pile of bank cards made her feel confused, pulled this way and that. She was packing for something she had agreed to do without thinking — as was the case with many things — in a place that she had thought would be snowy but was apparently hot, working on a project to commemorate some people who had died a long time ago.

She was distant and irritable before she left. While the devices that powered the wasted time were unremarkable, they were also familiar and safe. In the air, a little girl with thick black plaits ran screaming up and down the gangway, and the stale air filtered in and out of lungs as they piled the plane food into their mouths.

The terminus was unremarkably European, its only difference a language with symbols like archaic farmers' tools. A long, slow coach ride ensued, during which she spoke with her neighbour about London and how they passed the time there. The conversation was of pleasantries and vague mutual interest; between drowsy answers and endless road, her attention was tugged at by smatterings of gravestones.

Buildings in town rose and fell like the surfing of channels — all squat, sun-washed storeys and little warm-clime plants of a documentary about a place far away. Bullet holes peeped through the walls, and she couldn't shake the feeling they were on the set of a war film. Everything was rendered in the technicolour itch of an imagined life.

They had to walk to where they were to sleep. Night encased the trickling gravel pathways, noise barely discernible from the thronging creatures of the greenery. The woman at the door had no English but drew each new arrival into the valley of her breasts where they shifted, unused to such informality, below the alp of unbridled white hair. After an unpacking of the territorial spill of products onto surfaces, they were driven through the darkness to eat. The warm air made her feel full, so she drank far too much and danced to a language with no words.

She woke groggily, unused to a day that seemed so eager to begin. The fact that everything looked different made it seem unnecessary. In the tumbledown hall a breakfast of big, wet fruits and freshly baked bread had been provided; she declined but bought cigarettes which cost a handful of those foreign throwaway coins and sat outside, pulling the smoke into her body, until the adults took to the stage to describe the town, its history and their place within. The talks were long, interrupted by native speakers whose broken English prickled a dull ache in her skull. It was easier to look at the way a nose had broken with the searing cartilage welded back onto the face, or the chasms in the walls, or the swerving of the great, black insects.

At lunch they explored. Each new turning offered the same clustered street where a house had perished, scorched walls and roofs seeking a neighbour's relative comfort. That afternoon they curved further up the landscape, along the thirsty bank of a spent river to its apex; a spring whose progress had been stilted by the phantom government and was now a dry disappointment of rock. She had worn her bikini under her clinging dress and felt annoyed, counting the hours until she'd return to her room, away from the scorpions and the snakes and the landmines.

She dwelt among problems in England, sore as sunburn when seen from a distance. On a day when the ether sprawled like a week-old bruise, they travelled to the lake. Unchlorinated water coruscated from bank to bank, and with a morbid curiosity, she checked the bed for teeth or scraps of bone. Reclining, as the breeze coerced rivulets round her feet, she was nudged by the idea that there was a story to be found here, too far to swim with neglected muscles. As the week pressed on, it was suggested that she visit a memorial site for all those people who had died a long time ago. A dusty car arrived as transport and they drove through little towns that looked like model villages, only burnt in places, dusted with the little graves.

Just when the bluffs and spurs of land promised to stay as they were, a palisade burst up along the road. The speed of the car and the bars hummed together; like a fist of crumbs hurled at pigeons her eyes were startled and blinked like the rapid beating of wings. Thousands of white stones stooped and curved in a

161

great semicircle and she thought of this country, and its constellation of graves as pilgrims resting as they slouched toward this breathless, blinding place. As she left the stuttering car she could feel the play of a fountain, hear the shuffle and stop of feet beyond the fence. She was led left but right through the meandering traffic and then a small chain-link gap, heretofore eclipsed by the prettiness of the memorial site. They walked through a warehouse district, away from the teeming world behind. Smashed windows lost their dystopian thrill and hung like old, black wounds in the brickwork. Ever-present lurked a corrugated stench, clinging to the nooks of this unlit place.

She was marched to an echoing gallery. The walls were neatly hung with pictures and captions, information clear and precise. It offered no agenda other than to tell the truth: so informal as to isolate the words from their meanings. She wasn't afraid to stand close and read the little print, inoculated as she was by her status as a bystander. Tourist. Voyeur. But as she made her way along the edges something snuck through the trappings of language. A trickle at first, enough to whet the reluctance of many gauche years. Then harder: it churned behind the mounted photographs, broiling, dissolving the safety of time, of distance. And half-way through that grave and monstrous room, it shattered any resolution and she was torn open and stood, unprotected in a deluge that seeped from every single thing.

And she forgot to check herself and cried with other lonely travellers who knew now with a newborn's instinct that the world was bad. She moved perhaps for the first time beyond herself, and saw mothers torn from their husbands and sons when all their breaking bodies had wanted was to shield them from harm, and they had failed but so again had everything; nature begot nature and clawed a rift in itself, giving men the weapons to rend the very fabric of whatever they were.

She returned from there to shiver in a ghostly room; the ceiling cradled the poor light and she felt like she was floating in some nether-world. The universe so deep and gently dreaming and her so wide awake, for how would humans sleep again with death an aphorism on the lips of some fool? When she did sleep, she saw her father, butchered and bleeding, and woke abruptly with a child's need to see her family, and to kiss them while she could, their permanence as shaky as her hands. She felt alive with terror and tip-toed through a jagged world to find something, anything to cling to.

On the balcony of their little house, the hoary night spun indigo tresses round her head, full of scatterings of stars more real than when they had actually burnt. Some rich, foreign music floated up from deeper in the valley, tendrils of notes curling like the ivy on the balustrade. The air was lustre as if every flower had opened early and beat out a heady pollen. She breathed. She drank the life around her, welcomed it unquestioningly for perhaps the first time.

She went from there to listen to the world and its people. This raped place still clung to its torn dress, but beneath the ravaged garment something she could only describe as spirit — ebullient, breast bared — had tended to it for the broken years afterwards. She met a man who had walked down a road of human bones. His friends had died here. He said he wished the same for those responsible, then turned away with guilt, as if in that hushed and choking utterance he had sustained some cycle. Their kind, wordless host had lost her family. They let her hold them for as long as she liked when she came up to say her silent, eloquent goodnight. The young, without fathers and brothers, danced and sang and created with a fierce, unquenchable passion.

In that place, she learnt to invert herself, like a piece of origami whose meaning was never clear until that last, deft tug. There were hate and fear, yes, but those could only amount to ashes and dust and out of those the purest shoot had fought and flourished. As the days drew in the universe shucked its veil, and all around them, every patch of life was trembling.

London flickered in neat little squares as the plane descended. She couldn't quite describe the time away; in its most superficial form, she felt that she was *born*.

As the train slid from the station the platform melted into fresh snow, all tangerine-pink and purple ochre, and in that bursting summer's eve the sprawl lay incandescent. Into the night—dim now… but getting brighter.

Stations

E J Jennings

Mum stood nervously but collected on the platform, her eyes lightly darting, resting, darting and then resting on each detail of the Chinese hubbub around us. Until now her thirst for travel had been amply quenched with a day return to London in reserved window seats with sockets near the toilets on the quiet carriage of a South-Western Railways train. Never at a table, though. Not when travelling alone. Far too much risk of riff-raff.

I'd bunk off work to meet her at the station, and we'd saunter north over the Thames to a museum or two, then lunch with something fizzy, a gentle stroll around Knightsbridge and a potter back to Waterloo, the Marks and Sparks, where she'd buy her usual mini Sauvignon complete with handy plastic glass, finding once again her seat by the window in the quiet carriage, contentedly beaming at a day well spent. Simply that, in those days, passed for adventure.

And yet there she was, and here we were, in the farthest reaches of western China, awaiting our train to Tibet.

It was a huge shock, an overwhelming new reality, to step aboard this foreign vehicle destined for distant lands we'd never touched but so often dreamt of. Everything about it invaded our senses. We stood, rooted to our spot on the platform by bodies belonging to heads boasting thick black glossy hair that buzzed around us, talking, shouting, gesticulating, knowing much more than we did of what was to come. Steaming cartons of noodles passed over our heads, menthol cigarettes were blown in our faces, babies with gaping holes at their bottoms where nappies should be, hovered over bins by their Mothers whispering 'sss, sss, sss' in attempts to empty their bowels before departure.

We boarded with this flow of humanity, a choiceless act, swept forwards with the hordes, slightly clammy and person-scented as the setting sun cooled a day's sweat on their skin. Elbows were sharpened as the doors hissed open, anxiously twitching in their angst to find space, some certainty of place, a safe little territory aboard the crowded little vessel that would pierce through the borders of a kingdom that once flourished in independence, now subdued through invasion. Invasion and multiplication.

I glanced at Mum to check on her state, but she was bright and calm, radiant even, in the face of such bodily intrusions, accepting these truths as part of our journey, a necessary path that one takes in the course of a life that is lived to its maximum enrichment.

Inside, the train was blues and greys: steel walls, aluminium frames, navy plastic mattresses, grey Formica tables, plastic cups. The sense that many bodies had been there, resting on these hard, uniform beds, pacing these narrow-windowed corridors, looking out at the world as it passed them by, cognisant of change and of movement, of time passing by through passive hopeful eyes.

Our cabin door rattled open revealing four berths and a middle-aged Chinese couple, already installed in the bottom two bunks. The woman sat on the side of hers, feet swung onto the floor, fussing with creams for her night-time ritual, fetching and returning little pots and small sticks from a clear plastic bag, daubing light green mush here and pale pink wax there. The man lay on his back staring up at the top bunk, one hand resting on the taught tanned skin of his bloated stomach, index finger playing in the shallows of a deep round belly button, stretched from an excess of beer and oil and pork. Vacant in expression, he blew smoke rings into the small space above his head, despite the universally recognisable 'No Smoking' signs stuck prominently on the door.

I glanced at Mum again, the stickler for rules, the queen of discipline, the immediately irritated by inconsideration. But she shrugged, unusually accepting, apparently unphased by small niggles in the grand scheme of this journey. I briefly marvelled at this sudden arrival of equanimity before gently jolting, along with the other thousand or so souls, into phutt-phutt motion as the train began the journey.

We took the top bunks, me leaping athletically, she cautiously climbing the ladder, aware of the approaching Big Seven-Oh. She had her special Tibet-trip slippers on, fleecy on the inside, with good grip and a splash-proof outer layer. Her new Tibet-trip pyjamas were looking good, a little flappy around the knees admittedly, but with a fetching plaid colour scheme to accommodate less washing.

She'd brought a little eye mask too, and some earplugs just in case, all neatly packed in her little Tibet-trip bag bought from the chemist down the road from her old quarryman's cottage in her rural Dorset town.

I listened to her breathing as we dozed that first night. It was an old habit of mine, stretching back a decade through all our Mumsie-Daughter trips. I loved the idiosyncrasy of her sharp little puffs. In she would breathe and then hold it a little, pursing her lips, making the most of the life-giving air, before a gently jolting 'PPppeeerrffffff' of her out-breath, as her lips broke their seal and the air was returned to the space around her face. My breathing joined with hers and our joint gentle rhythm fell in with the train's phutts, clunking along the tracks, sighing and listing, as it edged its way uphill to that plateau of land, the uppermost world, where earth and sky say a final hello.

They had warned us about altitude sickness, of course. They had said that it was unpredictable and that there was little one could do to avoid it. No amount of training or good diet could guarantee an escape from its grips. But of course, we did all the research and prepared ourselves as best as we could. I'd bought Mum some Nordic Walking sticks for Christmas, hoping that their shiny strength would give her the courage to get out and about more, socialise with other active types, that sort of thing. And she had duly got out, joined a weekly beach walk with other 'crinklies', as we called them. She didn't enjoy it exactly, but it was all worth it in preparation for our trip. We'd invested in little oxygen tanks too, and those bands that push special points on your wrists, all the anti-nausea gear we could carry, really.

We got away with it for ages. We felt invincible waking up that first morning on the train! The scenery was changing, gently merging realities as we gradually left civilisation behind. Smoggy urbanity changed to settled suburbia, changed to ramshackle shacks, changed to factory stacks, changed to scrubland polluted, changed to fields, then sandy fields, then pebbles, then rocks and then inclining up through the rocks, round the hills, cut into sides, tiny homes, roadside children with gritty faces and sticky rice in their small clutching hands.

Mum was glued to the window, lying in her top bunk with the scratchy blue curtain pulled back behind her head as she craned to see where our journey was taking us. I kept a sharp watch for signs of the sickness. It was no small feat, taking a risk-averse sixty-nine-year old to Tibet. I felt responsible, knowing that if worst came to worst, I would be the one to carry us out of there. Maybe physically. I imagined the great explorers, in the face of catastrophe, putting friends on their backs and walking for days to reach water and medicine. I would do that for her. I would do anything for her.

We blithely continued upwards, phutt-phutting and chomp-chomping on noodles from pots with small shreds of green posing as vegetables and small chunks of brown with no relation to real meat. It was food for the institutionalised, both vile and bland, so we cracked out our British supplies early: the dried apricots and almonds, ready salted Pringles and Mr Kipling lemon slices, scrounging some hot water for a cup of PG Tips in her large orange flask kept going from the 80s. We made the trip our own, nibbling on the familiar though rarely hungry amidst the torpor of accepted immobility.

Suddenly the scenery changed dramatically. The steady rolling sparseness upped in intensity as the earth began rupturing, great brown jagged peaks screaming up from the ground, covered in trillions of sharp shale pieces, varying in size, layered over and over and over each other like sheets of shiny skin around a limb but each layer fractured and piercing and shifting at the slightest of forces. They were impassable those mountains, I felt sure of it. Even for the greats. There was nowhere to find purchase in that depth of moving shale. You might place one foot forward and feel hope from the brief stability that comes when a temporary platform forms from the chance compaction of those tiny little shards, but as you lifted your rear boot your front foot would slide from under you, the forward momentum pitching you down, cutting your palms on the razor rocks that amassed and pressed in around you. They were impassable, at least on foot, but not for the train. The train kept moving, phutt-phutt, through the gaps, finding the arteries to weave through the landscape, up and up and up, the air getting thinner, our blood working harder, the challenge increasing for us to stay vital.

Mum had rolled away from the window now, eyes closed, lying on her back with her hand resting delicately on her stomach. I could see her chest rising and falling with a greater sense of strain, her upper ribs jutting out further than her stomach as her diaphragm tightened with building anxiety.

She wasn't feeling well, she said. She had suddenly started to feel sick, her heart was thudding, her sweat was creeping. I kept calm and stayed strategic. Here was the Ziploc bag with the tablets and oxygen and wristbands and water. Lots of water. Stay hydrated. She complied with my ministrations, so much meeker than usual, her eyes somehow larger, more moon-like. Had she lost weight? Not this quickly, surely. It had only been one day on the train of nibbling on not much. One night and today.

I wouldn't worry yet, there were many things to try before the real worry kicked in.

We called for help some hours later, the nausea now over-powering and the Chinese couple long gone, in search of the food cart and some respite from the troubles of these unfortunate tourists. They didn't want to smell the sick or hear the groans. It's not easy to be around the ill and infirm.

The help arrived in response to my calls: one senior and two assistants, but they didn't speak my language. Or I didn't speak theirs. We were talking life and they were talking technology, solutions, fixes. They were uniformed in blues and greys, light blue short-sleeved shirts under light grey aprons, with little shiny badges, their names and titles pinned to their fronts. This is who I am, my role, I inhabit this space on this earth with this name that I have on my badge on my shirt. I am qualified to know what you need. Plastic gloves came out, snapped onto hands that touched my Mum's wrists and her forearms, searching, for where to put the needles and tubes. Our Ziploc was long gone, no more ginger capsules for us; it was time for chemicals, the strong ones. Mum was on a bottom bunk now, lying back on the blue plastic mattress with large white pillows and a light blue knitted blanket layered over starched white sheets. Everything smelled like metal and bleach. She looked serene, but scared, but calm, but accepting. She had never thought the chemicals would work, but she took the chance anyway, the chance to live, allowing the hope that after the worst there might be a better. That her future did not only hold worse and worse alone.

We continued together to the end of the earth, our bodies both adjusting to accommodate the changes. She often slept soundly, her little puffs coming and receding in beautiful regularity, the pursing still keeping that breath in her lungs just a few seconds extra, more molecules to exchange.

I left our adjacent doors open those nights, listening to her breath from my bed in her spare room. Sometimes I would stand naked at the full-length mirror. In the still of her rest, I'd put the bedside lamp on low and cast gentle warm shadows on the softly furnished room, smoothing the sharp angles of my shoulders and hips. I'd gaze blankly at the tall, wiry athletic body reflected back at me. It had always been strong and lithe, not feminine exactly, but taught and sprung and ready. But those nights it looked haggard, weak and thin, riddled with the trauma of unexpected journeys. I would wonder where the sadness was going. Was it stored in me somewhere? Did I have an inner limit? Could I find grief in my sinews if I cut them up and looked? Can my body survive this? Can her body survive this? How do we know when the damage has exceeded our body's own natural capacity to heal?

She phoned with the news as I walked over Blackfriars Bridge, on a short break in London to pop into the office.

'I'm afraid that it's not what we hoped for, my darling.'

There are semi-circular stone booths on that bridge. Probably put there for the tourists, they jut out away from the busy road towards the Thames and have a bench running around the inside. I moved to the nearest one and picked a spot to sit amongst the cigarette butts and takeaway cartons.

Our journey was ending now. Just one station left.

The Authors & Contributors

Gareth Cadwallader: Eliot said that Donne was, 'constantly amalgamating disparate experience…forming new wholes'; easy for Eliot or Donne—not so easy with just a spoonful of talent to work with. My first novel, Watkins & Son is published by Wet Zebra. My play, Cleopatra, has been performed at the Kings Head and Hope theatres in Islington. Madame Manet and Blood-Crossed have been performed at the Tabard in Chiswick. I'm currently working on a collection of short stories based loosely around *The Fall*. When off the field of combat, I work with entrepreneurs in London helping them grow their businesses.

Kennedy/Ken Coombs: I'm a 22-year old trans musician. I have been writing for 15 years and I started to help me cope with my parents' divorce, but it has grown to be a strategy for all emotional situations. I am originally from Eastbourne, East Sussex but I am currently residing in Weymouth, Dorset waiting to move to Hampshire. I have just recently started to get noticed because of a song based on my transition from female to male. In

177

February 2018 I was awarded the b-side TCFT Young Artist's Bursary.

Harrison Evans is a committed techie: the future is always coming! He read astrophysics before taking up a career as a full stack developer and is now heading for the nebulously exciting world of blockchain. When not writing code he loves drumming, reading & writing & watching sci-fi, rowing and learning…anything really.

S A Finlay published her first novel, *Carnaval*, with WriteSideLeft last year. It took her a few years because she was recovering from a Creative Writing Masters. She's written a lot of (some good, some average) poetry, been runner-up and longlisted in major poetry & short fiction competitions and is currently working on a cyberpunk novel that features the stories *Paradise by Numbers* and *Sawtooth Waves*.

Geoffrey Frosh, at school, long ago, an irritating jokester, a constructor of wayward narratives. Gainfully occupied, for nearly forty years, illuminating shady corners as a maker of images…Now back to word play…which feels, somehow, fresh and new.

Robert Golden: I've created many photo-stories, written/directed over forty documentaries, two feature films and worked as a director of photography/director on nine hundred TV commercials. I've written three plays, forty film-scripts, and many poems and essays about photography, politics and culture. In the last few years I've been teaching about Democracy as well as about photo-storytelling.

Olly Goodall is a London-based writer and content producer. When not writing copy as a wage-slave for clients, he writes short stories and poems. Interested in memory, light and empathy, his writing features in several UK publications.

Siobhan Harrison has an irksome habit of brandishing her pen as she says to baffled listeners, 'oh remember *that* line in *that* novel/poem?' She set up WriteSideLeft in 2017. It's her own wannabe Hogarth Press for the 21st Century. She depends on irony; so, she also works in Excel helping micro businesses survive. This is her first outing as an anthologiser.

E J Jennings writes through a necessity of catharsis, in attempts to understand and process the intensity of her relatively short life to date. She's about to start living in a van, with the intention of creating a nomadic, literary, soul midwifery sort of a life.

Maisie Kitton: I'm 17, I work part time in a Kiosk at West Bay and am currently doing an English Language and an English Literature A-Level (alongside a Creative Writing EPQ) at the Sir John Colfox Academy and Beaminster joint Sixth Form. I've been reading ever since my early years at primary school, but only began to start properly writing in year 8 when my English teacher told me I had a knack for it. Now I get told I write far too much by my friends! The *Wolves* stories are excerpted from my first novel of the same name.

Elise Ruby: Rather than allow mental health issues to be a mire, I try to find forms to accommodate depression, anxiety and OCD. I'm interested in the disconnect fuelled by technology, the public sector and the ways we self-medicate. Oh, and I have a burning desire to impress my dad.

Bardy Thomas: a slave and story-teller thought to have dwelt in Islington in the late 20th and early 21st centuries. Some authorities cite a prestigious career in the Theatre.

Acknowledgments

This anthology would not have been possible without the forbearance, talent, and trust of the authors, the help, encouragement, and spontaneous blind support of Caroline Grey, Deborah & Ady Goodall, Robert Golden, Tina Ellen Lee, and Annie Wheatley, of course, my family, and the sage, witty, and eminent Bernard Richards.

SAH 2018

WriteSideLeft

2018

www.writesideleft.com